Edward J. Kuntze, G.P. Putnam & Son

The Mystic Bell

a wonder story for young people

Edward J. Kuntze, G.P. Putnam & Son

The Mystic Bell
a wonder story for young people

ISBN/EAN: 9783337369255

Printed in Europe, USA, Canada, Australia, Japan

Cover: Foto ©Andreas Hilbeck / pixelio.de

More available books at **www.hansebooks.com**

A WONDER STORY FOR YOUNG PEOPLE.

NEW YORK:

G. P. PUTNAM & SON, 661 BROADWAY.

1869.

CONTENTS.

————o————

CHAPTER I.

NCE upon a time there lived a king and queen. This sounds familiar, for thus should a well-told nursery story begin; but to give you a better idea of how long ago it was that the following extraordinary events occurred, let me add, that had your great-great grandmother's great grandmother's grandmother told the tale, she too would have said: Once upon a time there lived a king and queen in the interior of Asia, whose domains bordered on the east on King Lion's realms, on the north on King Eagle's empire, and on the south on unknown countries. Our king loved warfare as a pastime, according to the fashion of those days; and so he carried on a continuous war with his neighbors, King Lion and King Eagle. This king and queen had a little baby, a wonderful boy, such as was never born before. He was the handsomest prince day ever looked upon, he was the strongest child any nurse ever carried in her arms; but all this was nothing compared with his wisdom. This wonderful baby when he had scarcely left the cradle actually understood the language of the animals. But this was not all: his nurses unanimously assured the whole astounded country that he would roar like a lion, howl like a wolf, sometimes twitter like a starling, and again hoot like an owl. Whenever he heard a dog bark, he listened attentively, and bow-wow-wow came his answer, whereto the dog made a reply; and thus Prince Armurat (that was his name) carried on a conversation in the bow-wow-wow language. In this way he talked with all the animals in their different tongues and dialects. And, strange to say, all this he did before he could speak the human language.

Far, far away in the woods, where even the daring hunter never ventured, lived a hermit—nay, a couple of hermits ; this may sound strange, but remember we have now entered a country full of marvels and wonders. This extraordinary couple of hermits had no children, but very much desired to have at least one, and morning and night they prayed to their God to send them either a little son or daughter.

Kings and queens are familiar to you, I suppose, and therefore I did not say anything about their appearance ; but hermits are not often portrayed in pictures, and therefore I will tell you how they looked. They were a foot taller than our tallest people are nowadays ; the husband's head was formed like a sugar-loaf, his eyebrows were shaggy and ash-colored, his eyes deep set and jet black, and inclined toward the root of his nose, like a Chinaman's ; but his beard was wonderful to behold : it was snow-white, and reached down to his knees, and he would always wipe his chair with it (that is, the block he used to sit on) while taking his meals. In figure he was lank and long. His wife was the reverse—inclined to be fat ; her long sandy hair, carefully braided, almost touched the ground when she walked ; and her feet would have raised the envy of a mandarin lady, so small and delicate were they. Her

1*

nose peeped timidly out from between two rosy hills of cheek; and as she had no eyebrows, her large blue eyes appeared singularly unprotected, and like two smiling forget-me-nots.

Had the Greeks seen this couple perhaps they would have called them Mr. Pan and Mrs. Dryad. But yet they did not exactly look like these demi-gods of fair Greece. They probably had names, however, which have got lost upon the road of time, and we may as well, for convenience sake, call them Mr. and Mrs. Pan.

One fine evening, when Mr. Pan was wending his way home after his day's work, which had been to assist some tender aspiring vines to climb stout and lofty trees, happy in his mind, as a man feels who is conscious of having spent his day in useful benevolent occupation, his ear was struck by a singular tingling sound, unlike anything he had ever heard before. He recalled to his memory the voices of all the animals, birds, and other creatures so familiar to him, but in vain. Although very hungry and tired, he said to himself, " I must go and see what that is ;" and so he went on in the direction from whence the remarkable sound came. Swarms of insects were evidently attracted by the same cause ; as he went on, numbers of butterflies, beetles, mosquitoes, gnats, bees, and flies passed him in hurried flight, and coming from every point of the compass, gathered at one spot, where the river with a sudden bend left the woods to sport in the flower-studded meadow. But only imagine his astonishment, when, entering the bramble hedge which decorated a group of palm-trees, he saw a huge black beetle mounted on a purple toad-stool, and a beautiful butterfly on a live turtle, ringing a sky-colored bell by means of shining spider-web cords. Locusts and grasshoppers filled the velvet lawn and joined in a wonderful dance, performing the Orthoptera ballet. All their cousins looked on in rapturous delight, hardly able to keep their feet still. Above the bell a number of gnats were whirling around in a circle, singing:

> Tingle, tingle, tingle!
> In company and single!
> Sing the joy of little fairy!
> Sleeping in the blooming prairie!
> Tingle, tingle, tingle!
> In company and single!

After looking on a while, our friend the hermit shook his head in bewilderment and went home. The mysterious tune of the bluebell had singularly moved the heart of the old unsophisticated man, and more than once he stepped out of his way for fear of killing some insect that crawled in his path.

Yet more surprise was in store for him that evening. Coming home his wife received him with a big bundle in her arms, apparently made up of furs and leaves. Her face was radiant with joy, and on his asking what was in the package, she held it up to him, saying: "Do you not see, sir?"—"O ho!" he exclaimed, "what a nice little monkey! where did you find it? but don't tie it up in such a cruel way. Does he eat apples?" and taking a fine one out of his pocket, he added, "there, my little monkey, take it, if you can get your hand free." But a hard rap from Mrs. Pan's plump hand made that apple of discord fall to the ground and roll out of sight, and Mrs. Pan's melodious voice sang out, "You ought to be ashamed of yourself, to call our little daughter a monkey; the Great Spirit sent her this very morning for our special care."

The poor man was all astonishment. Never having seen a baby before, and not recollecting having been one himself, how could he tell what it was? He looked at it gravely a while, and then said: "It isn't like you, it can't be like me; what a mystery!" Tingle, tingle, tingle was heard, like the sound of a tiny silver bell. "Oh dear! oh dear! what shall I do? there it is again!"

cried Mrs. Pan. "It is the same music she made when first I took her in my arms."

Mr. Pan looked earnestly into the baby's staring eyes, and murmured, "The same queer noise that I heard in the meadow," and, putting his ear close to the bundle, he added, "It comes from her heart;" and it drew him irresistibly toward the little creature. With tender affection he looked into her blue eyes, and the little thing began to smile. Then he kissed her, and she laughed; he kissed her again and again; he tossed her high up in the air, and sang to her in his croaking voice, his feet beating time quicker and quicker, until between them they performed the Orthoptera ballet, a dance that would have done honor to any Pan of antiquity.

Till then Mrs. Pan had been looking on in mute astonishment, wondering what had come over her husband, who was usually so grave and earnest; but at this outburst she got frightened about the safety of her baby, and ran after him screaming and calling for the child. But Mr. Pan in a fit of frantic joy leaped over brooks and rocks and fences, and would probably have bounded over the house, if that had not, fortunately, been a cave.

The inmates of the woods had gathered around to

see what was the matter, the magpie having sounded the trumpet of alarm. The parrot tribe was the first on the spot, and forthwith commenced the noisiest kind of dispute; some declaring that *he* was crazy, and the opposition maintaining that *she* was. The grave owls looked on in silence, pondering over the origin of species; the peacocks stood in brilliant array, not that they cared much about what was going on, but they thought it a good opportunity to show off. The singer tribe, led by Mrs. Nightingale, sang a welcome chorus; the crows and starlings, too, had a great deal to say; and as everybody was anxious to be heard above everybody else, there arose such a deafening noise, that nobody could be understood at all. Tingle, tingle, tingle—dead silence—and the infant smiled. The storm was allayed; then all the creatures began singing a beautiful chorus full of harmony, in honor, they said, of the arrival of their little queen, and then they suggested a name for the little girl.

After this quartet Mr. Pan gave the little darling to his wife, who gathered moss and dry leaves, and turning a table in the cave upside down, laid the little stranger in it, and there she very soon fell into a sound sleep. The birds immediately dispersed, talking only in a whisper, for fear of disturbing the slumbers of their queen.

And now, going further into the story, I will give you the quartet, so that from it you may learn the name of our little heroine. The song was found among Prince Armurat's lotus-leaves :—

Hail ! fair Zuleika ; hail,
  Lily of the valley !
Child from a higher sphere,
  Princess Zuleika !

All in a chorus join,
  Sing : hail Zuleika !
Shout it from dawn to night,
  Sweet, sweet Zuleika.

All of us promise thee—
  Hear it, Zuleika !—
Thy body-guard to be,
  Lovely Zuleika.

Always live happily
  With us, Zuleika ;
Never depart from us,
  Fairy Zuleika.

Since that little puss (as Pan in his rough way used to call her, by way of endearment) had arrived they both agreed that they had been a great deal happier than before. If ever there occurred a difference of opinion between them, as there always will in every

well-conducted household, the ringing of that tiny bell
reached their ears, and they immediately joined hands
and made a compromise.   There was now no more a
doubt but that the mysterious ringing proceeded from
the heart of our Zuleika.   The mother had detected
the faintest outline of a tiny bell where the heart lay
beating, which little spot would quickly move up and
down whenever the ringing was heard.

Zuleika grew to be a wonderfully beautiful child.   I
cannot describe how beautiful she was when five years
old ; and if you could mould into one all the beautiful
girls that have been described in all the romances
written within the last four centuries, the result would
be far below what she really was.   Where she got
such beauty from I cannot imagine, neither could Mr.
or Mrs. Pan.

It was charming to see how all nature did homage
to that good and beautiful child.   Everything seemed
to love her, and take care not to do her any harm.
Whenever she wandered about in the woods barefooted,
which she had to do, as her father did not know how
to make shoes, the ferns would spread their long downy
leaves flat upon the ground before her, so that she
might step upon them and keep her feet from being
hurt by the thorns and stones.   The brambles and

woodbines would raise their tangled leaves and branches at least a foot above her head, and so her path would be through archways of fruits and flowers. No hawk would ever think of killing a sparrow when she was near, and if ever one were caught by her in the act, he would sit down quite crest-fallen, as if repenting his evil doings. The greatest task of our Zuleika was to govern the refractory empire of ants. They would constantly wage war among themselves, and make slaves of their prisoners. Those with the lighter skins were evidently the more powerful, and had succeeded in subduing the weaker black tribes and making them do their work, for which they gave them nothing but mildew. As soon as the bell in her heart gave the alarm of a battle close by, she would hasten to the spot, drive the assailants away, and restore the captives to their liberty.

One day, when Zuleika was taking a stroll in the fields, she met a partridge mother, followed by her brood of little children. Dame Partridge, in her motherly pride, paraded her whole family in a row before Zuleika, who had seated herself in the grass. When every one of the piping things had been inspected, and received its praise for a special beauty, they were allowed to play in the grass.

But while she was enjoying their droll tricks, Zuleika's bell announced the approach of an enemy. The child looked around, but saw only a huge snake winding its way toward the playground. Zuleika feared no danger, but when with the approach of the reptile the alarm rang louder, she rose to run away. When Mother Partridge, who had called all her children around her, perceived this, she began to lament, and looked up to Zuleika in great distress. Our little heroine, understanding the appeal, said, " Be quiet ; I will protect your children ;" and taking a stick she put herself in a defensive attitude. The snake halted, and raising its flattened head, prepared for a leap. Zuleika aimed a blow at her, but missed. Quick as lightning the snake leaped upon the child, winding her coils around the slender body, and darting out her cloven tongue. " Help, help !" cried Dame Partridge in the greatest agony, brushing the grass with drooping wings.

Tingle, tingle, tingle rang the bell, in the very tune which the gnats had been singing ; and now the snake began to tremble in turn, its head began to droop, its coils relaxed, and it prepared to hide away among the bushes, when a stork, attracted by Dame Partridge's cry for help, seized it by the throat, and after twisting its neck, buried the body in his own stomach.

Whenever Zuleika took a bath in the river, the very fishes came swimming to kiss her feet. These signs resembled pinches more than kisses, she thought ; but knowing that this was fish-fashion, she politely acknowledged the compliment. Sometimes she would take up a fish and hold it in her lips, and oh ! how enchanted the little fellow became then ! It would flap its finny hands and tail, and show its cold-blooded enthusiasm in every possible way, until she laughingly threw it back into the water again. There it would be instantly surrounded by envious friends, longing to know what a kiss from fairy lips was like. Some of the sturdier fish would dive down to the bottom of the brook, praying cousin oyster to give them pearls for ornaments for the good Zuleika. The oyster, that habitual miser, never leaving his treasure for a minute, strange to relate, gave willingly ; and what was still more wonderful, others of their cousins, who owned beautiful houses, stepped calmly out of them, and asked cousin fish to give them to Zuleika as tokens of love and affection from the inhabitants of the river-bed.

But now let me tell you how our darling's seventh birthday was celebrated by her many friends.

Several days previous to her birthday, Zuleika perceived a peculiar commotion among her subjects (it

seemed as if all animate nature had submitted to the
choice of the birds, who had elected her queen).   Whispers and titters and all sorts of sounds were heard everywhere during the several nights preceding, and Mr.
and Mrs. Pan and Zuleika did not know what all this
could mean.   But on the morning of the seventh birthday everything was explained.   The dawn of day was
glorious, for the sun rose and peeped over the hill-tops
clear and bright ; not a single cloud was in his way ; the
bats had been busily at work all night, sweeping the
sky ; the moths had been engaged in collecting perfume
from the flowers for miles around, and now they sprin-
kled it all over and around the cavern.

No sooner did Zuleika show her head at the door,
than the whole Philharmonic Society of the feathered
tribe burst out into a most beautiful quartet, arranged
for this occasion by Skylark, composer to his majesty
King Eagle.   When this chorus was finished, the
Sarus, the stateliest of the cranes, offered his right wing
to Zuleika, and, proudly swinging his graceful neck
forward and backward, conducted her down to the river,
where she habitually went in the morning to bathe her
hands and face and her tiny feet.   There she found the
beavers had been at work, and had built a most beautiful archway, lined by a dozen peacocks with expanded

tails ; two fine lyre-tails stood upon opposite pillars ; and two cockatoos, in beautiful clear maiden-blush robes, with a coronet upon their heads and an exquisite collar around their necks, delivered a birthday address on the part of the three kingdoms. It was quite classical, written by the cardinal.

Thence the crane led her, through a woodbine covered passage, to a lovely little spot where she had never been before ; there the creatures had built a magnificent temple. Creepers with beautiful flowers were en-twined around each pillar ; the roof was decked with the most brilliant-colored feathers, which the parrot and humming-bird families had furnished ; garlands of polished shells, contributions from the maritime empire, together with rare festoons of pearls, corals, and amber, were swung with artistic taste around the glistening columns. The tailor-birds had sewed together a large flag from the leaves of red roses and white lilies, and on it they had embroidered "Zuleika" in big letters with the blue leaves of the cornflower.

In this temple the creatures had prepared a splendid banquet. Dog, cat, and rabbit, goose and sparrow, had all been eagerly at work to serve a regal repast ; and how they had succeeded you may judge, when I tell you that the tiny mice had been at work for several days transforming bushels of wheat into the finest flour, the woodpeckers had gathered figs and raisins, the squirrels brought almonds, the bees brought twenty pounds of choicest honey, the hens brought eggs. The ducks had made the dough, the geese kneaded it thoroughly; the cats had mixed the ingredients and made a rich plum-pudding, but the dogs protested against its being served up with burning brandy sauce, for fear Zuleika's dress might catch fire and the birthday festival be converted into a funeral scene. The little reed swallows even had contributed a dozen of their sprig nests; the pepper-eaters had picked a quantity of cocoa beans, from which the finest chocolate was prepared by the spoonbills. Some unmentionable animals came grunting, greatly elated with the result of their performance—a huge dish in the shape of a pudding, with a strong flavor. The goat, acting as head steward, would not let it go on the table; he declared it unfit to be eaten. This, of course, deeply offended the cooks, who got very angry, calling it calumny, and mean, contemptible envy; and to prove that the steward was prejudiced against them, they at once sat down and devoured their own pudding with indescribable relish.

The clever bees had built a nice table of empty

honey-combs right in the middle of the temple, around
which the moles had thrown up little heaps of earth
for the guests to sit upon.   At the upper end they had
made a bench large enough for three, which they covered with fresh moss.   To this seat mother goose, who
did the honors at the table, conducted Zuleika.   Two
glossy black squirrels, with lily-leaf aprons, stood as
waiters behind her; and very amusing it was to see
with what grace they performed their duty.   For in-
stance, you would see one of them dart like lightning
to the opposite end of the table, to fetch a cabbage-
leaf laden with strawberries, piled into a pyramid by
the starling, and place it before his mistress without
disturbing a single one of the berries.

His comrade would fill a convolvulus to the brim
with fresh-gathered dew from the honeysuckle, put it
on his head, and, throwing himself upon his knees before Zuleika, offer it to her without spilling a drop.
The brown plum-pudding, studded all over with almonds, and served upon a leaf from the Victoria Regia,
was pronounced the greatest success.   The chocolate
was handed around in tiger-lily chalices, and the cus-
tard in the flamingo egg-shells.

The centre of the table was ornamented with a fanciful structure, like a Christmas tree, covered with many

colored wax candles, and surmounted by a golden figure representing the bee queen; fantastic figures, cut out of a gray material like paper, and variously dyed, were suspended from its branches; this was the ingenious work of the great wasp family. Apart from the table was a platform upon which threescore crickets and as many locusts were seated, playing popular airs most indefatigably, while the party enjoyed the breakfast.

After dinner the stately crane took Zuleika to a green lawn close by, where a kind of stage had been erected. The moment Zuleika appeared on the lawn, leaning on the crane's wing, half a dozen baboons commenced making a deafening noise with drums and fifes, cymbals and shrill whistles. All the company flocked together in a great throng, preferring fun to feasting, only the ducks and crows remaining, for these gluttons had not had such an opportunity to indulge their appetites for a long time.

About a dozen spider-monkeys had got up a pantomime of a very original character. Among others, one of their feats consisted in catching hold of each other's tails and forming a long chain, when the monkey on each end would climb a pole, and thus raising the whole chain of monkeys from the ground, form a tight

rope, upon which a very clever monkey urchin performed extravagant dances. Another one would
drive a wheel-barrow over them, blindfolded, without
even a balancing pole. This was immensely cheered.
Some performed upon the swinging trapèze, literally
flying over the heads of the trembling assembly.
Some called this great fun, but others saw no fun in it,
and called it a torture. This finished the programme.
Zuleika shook the wings and paws of all her friends,
cordially thanking them for the pains they had taken
to please her, and then was escorted home by the
proud crane.

With rapturous delight, Zuleika related to her
parents the marvellous events of the day; they listened
to it quietly, and saw nothing strange in it, and only
thought it natural and proper.

But the old man began to think that his little fairy
ought no longer to live in the dingy cave, and selecting
a beautiful spot a short distance from the hermitage,
he built a nice little house with two rooms—one for
Zuleika, and one for his wife and himself.

Scarcely was the house boarded in, when the swallows flocked together and ornamented the ceilings
with fanciful masonry, which the cochineals painted
red. The spiders came with tapestry from their own

looms, and covered the walls with proofs of their great talent in this department of the arts.

Our little friend was almost beside herself with joy over this beautiful house; she danced around it, and ran in and out; her chief delight was to open and shut the door, and to look out of the window. Next to this she enjoyed the wonderful pictures on the walls, showing the fearful struggle between the spiders and the dragon-flies, which ended in the overthrow and capture of the latter.

Observing how clever all her friends were, Zuleika longed to be able to do something too, and one day she went to her mother and said, " Please, mamma, give me something to do, so that I may become as clever as my friends are."—" Go and play, my darling," said Mrs. Pan; " you are too delicately made; your father and I will work for you." But Zuleika replied, " That's why I am so delicate, because you will not let me work and strengthen my muscles; and I want to be strong. Please give me some work, mamma." But Mrs. Pan said no: it would make her sick; and that ended the matter for that time.

Zuleika went to play as she was told, but soon planned work for herself. She had often watched the yellow oreole weaving his basket-like nest from the outermost branch of a tulip-tree. She saw him first form a skeleton in the shape of an egg, cut off at the top ; then he took thin sticks and fibres, which he artfully intertwined with the ribs, bending them outward and inward alternately, just as the spiders weaved their tapestry. " I will try and make a basket for mamma," said the little girl to herself, "in which she can carry home fruit from the field." After some trouble she succeeded in weaving a nice basket. Her joy was great, and she ran home to her mother swinging her basket in triumph, and singing and shouting all the way.

Mrs. Pan could hardly believe her own eyes, when she found that her little daughter had accomplished something that never had been done before. And after that she was allowed to work as she pleased.

Thus years passed on, with all in the secluded valley in perfect happiness and harmony. Zuleika grew taller and more beautiful every year, and the mysterious melodies of the silver bell remained the faithful companion of her childhood, her reliable guardian.

Time, the only thing in this world that does not change, moved on then just as quickly, just as slowly as in our days. Times may change, but Time does not.

Seventeen years with their changes had passed by. Prince Armurat had grown from a child into a handsome youth, and had become an ardent hunter. Often was he seen on his Arab steed to plunge into the wildest and most desolate parts of the mountain, to hunt the tiger and the lion. On one of these occasions it happened that . . . Why, boys! what's the matter now? Why do you chuckle and look at me so archly, as if you knew already what was coming? You seem to think of course he will lose his way in the woods this time, and then suddenly meet with Zuleika, as is the custom in fairy stories, fancy stories, and every other kind of stories. Now let me tell you, my young friends, that when somebody is telling a story which you happen to know already, it is never proper, but always impolite, to show by signs—such as nodding your head, or getting restless upon your seat, or exclaiming, " Didn't I say so?" etc.—that it is familiar to you. Believe me, it spoils all the fun. And if what you supposed had really come to pass, I assure you I would say not a word more, but leave it to you to finish the story yourselves. But as, fortunately, it did not happen as you anticipated, I am still under obligation to proceed.

CHAPTER II.

THE OWL COUNCIL.

ELL, then, it so chanced that on the day aforesaid Prince Armurat had been very unfortunate in his hunt, for he had not, as usual, shot half a dozen tigers, two or three elephants, a brace of lions, or even a solitary bear; but, worse than all, he had missed the only shot he had—a stag. He rode towards home, much vexed and tired, when, suddenly leaving the forest, he heard great laughter and noisy merriment among the birds. It soon became certain that he himself was the object of this boisterous gayety. A magpie was entertaining the whole feathered company with biting sarcasms touching his royal person and his unfortunate hunt. The woods were ringing with laughter. There would have been no danger had the magpie satirized any other mortal being but Prince Armurat, who, as we

know, understood the language of animals and birds.
Stung to the quick, he seized his bow, placed the ar-
row, and was just about sending his rarely-erring
death-messenger into the heart of poor magpie, when
he was checked in his purpose by a slap in the face.
What unspeakable insult! Who could dare to inter-
fere with the wrath of a prince?

It appeared that at this critical moment another
magpie had perched himself upon his royal nose, and
by flapping his wings in the prince's face had covered
his eyes.

The next moment, however, leaving his nose and
alighting upon the nearest tree, he cried, "Mercy,
mercy, most illustrious Prince, for my poor husband!
He did not know that you are familiar with our language,
or he surely would not have spoken such insulting
words in your hearing. O Prince! if you will promise me never to persecute my dear husband, I will
make him give you what he always boasts of being his
greatest treasure—I am sorry to say. Gracious Prince,
I know you will consider yourself well compensated,
if you accept my proposition, for sparing the life of
a reprobate magpie, whom, alas! I love so much,
though I know he is not worthy of it, but he is such
a nice—"

And thus poor frightened Mrs. Magpie might have rattled on for an indefinite time, had not the Prince stopped her eloquent speech by accepting her proposition, provided Mr. Magpie made a satisfactory apology.

It was highly funny to hear the excuses of Mrs. Magpie's husband, they formed such a contrast to his speeches in the woods among the merry audience. At last, taking from under his left wing a very small and brightly polished nutshell, which he opened and presented to the Prince, he said, "Most Gracious Royal Highness, the ocean has not as many drops, nor its shores as many grains of sand, as I need words to express my gratitude ; receive here my dearest treasure. Dearly as I love the precious metal, not all the gold of Asia would buy this from me. It is the portrait of a most beautiful maiden—the handsomest the sun ever smiled upon. Cousin Stork, the eminent draftsman, drew it for me, as a special mark of friendship."

"Thanked be the gods, it's gone! Thanks to the gods, it's gone!" exclaimed jealous Dame Magpie, hopping and dancing from branch to branch. "All the gods be praised, he has it no longer!"

The Prince and his horse stood immovable, as if suddenly turned into a statue.

"Is this the portrait of a living mortal, and is she as beautiful as she is represented here?" exclaimed the Prince, awakening from his trance.

"Both, and much more so ; and if you please, your Royal Highness, I will escort you to the spot directly, that you may convince yourself," cried Mrs. Magpie, fearing lest her husband should offer his services. "It is only two hundred miles from here, and in less than five hours we can be there."

"Thank you," said Prince Armurat ; "I do not believe my horse can match you in a race, but I will be here again at four o'clock, when you shall be my guides thither, both of you. Mark the hour." Thus saying, he pricked the spurs into his horse's sides, and went off homeward.

Early the next morning Prince Armurat started for the place of rendezvous to meet the Magpie couple, leaving word at home that if he should happen to stay all night they need not be alarmed. He found the guides at their post, where they had been since the earliest dawn.

Pity the poor horse that had to satisfy the Prince's impatience by following the Magpies' flight ! Dead silence met them everywhere. Unusual silence reigned in the forest ; no sound was heard save the rapping of the passing wind, as he smote the trees, announcing the arrival of the sun. The Magpies were confounded; this was contrary to their life-long experience.

The mystery made them irritable, and the horse had to suffer for it. This latter individual could not see the necessity for running himself to death, and when on the second night the party had arrived within forty miles of the hermitage, he stubbornly refused to go another step before he had eaten a substantial meal and had a good sound sleep. It was then agreed that he should remain there, while the Prince should pass the night in the neighboring palace of the Duke Shuhu, Chief of all the Owls.

The Magpie knocked at the door; Barnowl, the porter, opened, asking who was there. "A good friend on an important mission to his Grace the Duke." "Hoo, too, hoo-oo! is it you-u-u?" cried the Barnowl, "to-wit, to-wit, you know, you know—you wait, you wait, you know, you know, ho, ho, ho, hoo-oo!" And with this he slammed the door right in the face of the bewildered Magpie, almost at his wits' end. The Magpies had often been employed by the Duke as confidential messengers in his private affairs, and had always been admitted without ceremony; therefore this treatment almost broke his heart. He went to his wife, reporting what had happened ; they at once set to work guessing, and ran through a long list of impossible impossibilities,

After a while Porter Barnowl returned, and beckoning to Mr. Magpie, cried, " Come in, come in, alone, alone, ho, ho, hoo-oo ! "

Entering the hall, the poor gossip's astonishment increased with every step. Walls and furniture were completely covered with raven-feather cloth, and every one he met was lamenting, and had three raven feathers in his left wing. That something dreadful had happened was certain. How humiliating that he and his wife should be ignorant of it—they who knew everybody's secrets, real or imaginary. The Barnowl is a discreet servant, and made no reply to Magpie's confused questions. He gravely said, " The Duke is holding private council, and anxiously awaits your tidings." Arriving at the council-room, he threw the door open, announcing—

" Sir Chattering Magpie."

What a scene did he behold ! We must really beg a thousand pardons of Prince Armurat, and, as we are in duty bound to call her, Lady Magpie, for leaving them outside in the dark yet a while, but we must take a look at this council-room.

Sir Chattering Magpie was conducted into a circular room with an arched roof, covered from ceiling to floor with the skins of black mice. Heads of small animals and birds were arranged in ornamental groups on different parts of the wall.

Facing the wall stood a kind of throne, raised a few feet above the floor, from the centre of which rose a polished ebony stick, with another one at the top crossing it horizontally, thus forming a Roman T. Narrow stripes of beautiful green snake-skin were twined around it at intervals, and from the ends of the cross-stick bunches of blue and purple beetles were suspended.

Upon this throne sat Shuhu, Chief of the Owls.

The curtains which formed the back of the throne were artfully made of blackbird feathers. Right and left of the Duke sat state dignitaries, twelve in all. Upon a crimson toadstool in the centre of the circle, formed by the state dignitaries and the throne, lay fifty glow-worms, diffusing a mysterious phosphoric light throughout the room, making it almost daylight for the Owl Council.

The Magpie trembled, and his feathers rose on end at this sight; he knew nothing of the existence of such a chamber. He soon learned that this was the secret hall of justice, and that the heads on the wall were those of criminals that had been executed on the spot, for offences committed against the mandates of the illustrious Duke.

"Welcome, Maggy," cried Shuhu; "you never came at a more opportune time. Be quick and brief in telling us what you know about our Princess."

"Princess!" cried Sir Chattering, "your Grace probably means to say Prince. Listen, then, illustrious Duke. Prince Armurat sends me with a message to your Grace, the short of which is, that he intends to do your Grace the honor to pass the night in your palace, darkness having overtaken him on his way to the fair Zuleika."

"Zuleika!" cried the Shuhu; "speak at once; where is she? what do you know of her?"

"Nothing, but that she lives safe and happy in the secluded valley," stammered Magpie; but when at this moment all the owls were staring fixedly at him, he almost fainted, but recovering himself, he asked, "Has anything serious happened to our darling?"

"Hoo, hoo-oo! are you feigning ignorance?" exclaimed Shuhu; "this looks suspicious, for it is incredible that you, gossip, should not know of her disappearance."

"I pledge you my knightly honor, I was not aware of

this awful occurrence! Can it really be true?" cried
Maggy.

"How now! I suspect your Prince has stolen our
dear Zuleika, and you were his helpmate. Am I not
right? And you have the audacity to show yourself
at our court? Is this a stratagem to mislead our
efforts to find her again? But you will not succeed.
Call in the guards; summon the Sheriff; this villain
must be executed on the spot, if he does not immediately reveal where Zuleika is hidden. Your head, Sir
Chattering Magpie, shall be nailed to the highest
battlement of Castle Shuhu, an example of our unspar-
ing justice, and a warning to all. Command High-
Sheriff Virginia Owl to drive this would-be Prince
Armurat into this sacred chamber, and here in our
presence shall he scratch out his royal eyes, and
from here he shall be dragged into King Lion's realms,
a prey for his tigers."

In vain did poor Maggy assert his Prince's innocence. Shuhu was in too great a rage to listen to
anything, and screamed till he was hoarse, "Revenge,"
and all the dignitaries echoed "Revenge!" which
word is synonymous in their language with justice.

The guards seized upon Sir Chattering and laid his
head upon the block; the Sheriff drew back his sleeve,

he sharpened his claw, and was just ready to wring
the supposed culprit's neck, when with a fearful crack
the door gave way, and in stepped Prince Armurat,
sword in hand, closely followed by Lady Magpie.

But why did the Prince enter the hall of justice in
such an unjustifiable manner? Lady Magpie has told
the story thus:

"Tired of waiting so long outside, I felt great *ennui;*
the Prince had seated himself upon a log, and was soon
lost in drowsy revery; I was looking about in order
to find somebody to gossip with, and seeing a footman
hastily leave the palace, I stopped him to ask a few
questions—not that I was particularly anxious about
finding out what was going on, but it might be useful
to know, and pass the time. But the footman angrily
pushed me aside, and cried, 'Out of my way; I am
sent for the Sheriff to execute that villanous Sir Chattering.'—'Why?' I screamed, almost fainting; but off
he was, and I flew to Prince Armurat, imploring him
by heaven and earth to save my husband's life a second
time. He at once responded to my appeals, stormed
the castle, broke down all the doors, and then appeared
in the presence of the Duke and his wise councillors."
Thus far Lady Magpie's narrative.

All stared, owl-fashion, at the intruder.

Sir Magpie took advantage of the general confusion caused by the Prince's sudden appearance, escaped from the Sheriff's claws, and fluttered upon the Prince's shoulder.

"In the name of justice I demand an explanation," cried the Prince, boiling with rage; "why are you mal-treating my guide, who would be a corpse now, but for my seasonable arrival? Answer, or tremble for the consequences."

The Shuhu's eyes grew unnaturally big, he turned pale under his feathers, and was sorely confounded how to answer the demand without compromising his dignity. Recovering his presence of mind he shouted, "Sit down, down; sit down, down!" Beckoning a servant to place a T-shaped stick at his right side, he stepped from his throne and conducted the Prince in person to his seat, entreating him to be calm; all would no doubt be satisfactorily explained.

After order was restored, and all seated except those that had no seats, Duke Shuhu resumed as follows:

"Listen to what I have to say, and answer con-scientiously. Whither have you taken Zuleika, Prince Armurat? King Eagle's empire has sworn to pro-tect her, and we will faithfully do it, cost it what it may."

"Do you allude to this young lady?" said the Prince, showing the miniature in the nutshell.

"The very same; but what a charming likeness! Who drew it?"

"Cousin Stork, the great artist," cried both Magpies at once.

"He shall be patronized by us; send him to the castle to-morrow."—"But what about Zuleika, Duke?" said the Prince; "this likeness and her name is all that I know of her, but I long to see the original of this picture, and this incident increases my interest. To tell the truth, I was on my way to the abode of the fair maiden with these two honest people (pointing to the Magpies) as my guides, when my horse became too fatigued to proceed, and we concluded to accept your hospitality for the night."

"You are really not the robber!" exclaimed the Shuhu. "No, indeed," rejoined the three travellers. "What is the meaning of all this mystery? Speak!"

At this declaration all the owls flapped their broad wings, opened their round eyes doubly wide, and a mournful "to wit, to wit; ho, ho, ho, hoo-oo," rang through the lofty hall.

"Hear me, Prince," said Bishop Snowowl, perceiving that the old Duke was too much affected to speak.

"Listen to me. This morning, when we held a cabinet meeting, Secretary Vulture was announced, begging for an immediate hearing. Ushered in by Barnowl, he said that our fair Zuleika had been foully kidnapped this morning, while bathing in the river, by unknown human creatures. Wild rumors circulated among our people, although reliable particulars had not been received yet.

"The order of the day was suspended at once, and we have been debating this calamity all day, and had just passed a unanimous resolution that something ought to be done, when the arrival of Sir Chattering was announced. We were convinced that he knew all the particulars of this crime and who the parties were, and had come to inform us. But when he, as we suppose, feigned ignorance, and somehow connected your name with Zuleika's in one sentence, and when he shortly after altogether denied all knowledge of the abduction of our beloved Zuleika, we concluded that he was an artful deceiver and an accomplice in the foul deed, and condemned him on the spot to be executed, as the magnitude of the supposed crime deserved."

"Thank you, my dear Bishop; well spoken," said Shuhu; "and now let us proceed with our council. I hope Prince Armurat will do us the honor to join it."

Another moment and the whole council were deeply pondering this fearfully intricate matter. Rap, rap, rap, re-echoed the walls of the black chamber of justice, and all the wise owl-heads turned with one jerk towards the door, and Barnowl came rushing in quite out of breath, on announcing a special messenger from his all-powerful majesty King Eagle, absolute sovereign of the Kingdom of Feathers. General rising and fluttering. "He desires to be admitted without delay, being, as he professes, the bearer of a verbal message to your Grace."

"Show him in, in; show him in, in," commanded Shuhu.

Gracefully and proudly Lord Noblefalcon advanced, bending his head towards the Duke, and then nodding familiarly right and left to the members of the council. Clearing his voice, he at once began: "Gracious Duke, our mighty Sovereign desires you and the learned council to appear immediately before him. Events of grave importance have occurred, and your wisdom is required. An abduction has been committed within his dominions."

"Zuleika, Zuleika, ho, ho, hoo-oo," was heard again and again within those sombre walls, while the councillors prepared for speedy departure.

"Dear Prince," said Shuhu, "if you are not too much fatigued, would ask the honor of your company to King Eagle's palace ; his Majesty's commands make it impossible for me to entertain you in my castle according to my wishes."

" My interest in the affairs of this charming lady is increasing rapidly, and I will deem it the greatest favor if you allow me to be your companion," was Armurat's reply.

Barnowl announced that the carriage was waiting. When the Prince walked out, arm in wing with Shuhu, he found an elegant carriage at the door, or rather a car shaped like a gondola, made out of butterflies' wings, and drawn by twelve flying foxes. The two vampire lackeys, and Horse-shoenose, the driver, looked very grim.

" Quite safe," said the Duke, when he saw the Prince hesitating to embark in this frail-looking craft, " quite safe ; our artisans are trustworthy people ; excellence of workmanship is their leading ambition."

" Shuhu ! " cried the Duke, crack went the whip, and off sped the foxes high above the clouds and the sleeping earth. Behind them followed the train of sage councillors, wrapped in their night cloaks.

The Prince, fatigued from the day's journey and the

excitement of the night, soon fell asleep, and therefore remembered nothing of this extraordinary journey; and when Shuhu pulled one of his long black curls he awoke just in time to notice the gentle lowering of the car in front of a magnificent building, lofty as an air castle. It was King Eagle's palace. This palace was built of semi-transparent material, not known to us now. Rows of columns hewn out of rock crystals supported the roof of onyx. Twenty amber steps led to the vestibule; twelve white falcons rushed down the steps to receive the guests; a regiment of hawks formed a defile through which they passed. The condor, Lord Chancellor, received them in the hall and ushered them into the throne-room, where King Eagle, advancing a few paces from his throne, welcomed the Prince and led him to a chair on the right of the throne; the Duke's seat was on the left. The sages occupied their customary seats, and while they hold council we will inspect the throne-hall.

The throne, from the platform upwards, was actually a live one, entirely made up of living birds of paradise. It was built after plans by the court decorator. From the base of the throne, at equal intervals, sprang a number of bamboo canes, arranged in a semi-circle, bent inward at the top, to form the roof. In

each cane a number of short sticks were horizontally
inserted ; upon these birds of paradise were perched
so close together, that the framework was entirely hidden under their beautiful feathers. To this office they
were appointed for life or during good behavior, King
Eagle even having no power to remove them. The
pilasters running along the walls were made of rubies
with lazuli capitals ; the ceiling consisted of blue jasper,
inlaid with stars of yellow amber. A frieze carved in
emerald, illustrating the deeds of the King's noble ancestors in the wars between the Eagles and Reptiles,
ran along the wall below the ceiling. Statues in
marble of heroes and philosophers stood here and there
in niches. Amongst them I will only mention that of
a beautiful swan. The grace of the undulating out-
lines ; the unaffected but inspired expression ; the sim-
plicity of conception ; the manly, vigorous execution ;
the massive, masterly treatment of the downy feathers,
told at once that it was conceived and executed by
one of those heaven-descended masters who are occa-
sionally sent on earth with special messages, to give a
painted idea of the sublime beauty and harmony of
the brighter spheres to the grovelling creatures below.

Now let us return to the council, and hear whether
their mighty wisdom has found out who stole Zuleika.

King Eagle, with a vermilion crown upon his head, ornamented with green and gold beetles, sits in grave earnestness, holding the feather sceptre of the empire. To the right sit his ministry, to the left the learned owl council, while the centre is occupied by both houses of the kingdom. Opening his thinly bearded beak, and shaking his ample royal robe, which made a number of feathers, like messengers of his sorrow and anger, fly in all directions, he burst out in a mournful " Keèack, keèack, keèack " (meaning " woe, woe is me "), to which the owls responded in a long-drawn " hoho, hoho, hoo-oo-oo ! " and the woodpecker tapped a roll upon a muffled drum. After this expression of sorrow the King began : " My Lords, Reverend and Honorable Gentlemen of the Empire, we have called you together to announce to you that an outrageous offence has been committed against our sovereignty, which is not only in itself a national calamity, but comprises a special calamity to every one of our subjects. Open your ears and hear ; the lovely Zuleika, our Fairy Ward, has been stolen from among us. Keèack, keèack, keèack ! "—" Ho-ho, ho-ho, hoo-oo-oo ! ", responded the owls, and " Bum, bum, bum ! " finished the woodpecker on his muffled drum. When all was quiet the King proceeded : " Vague rumors are afloat about the cursed perpetrator of so black a deed, but the one to which I give credence is, that Zamurang the magician is the villain. But all this is mere guess-work, and you are called together to devise means to recover our Fairy Queen. The illustrious council is opened ; my Lords and Gentlemen, to your duty. Keèack, keèack, keèack." " Ho-ho-hoo-oo ! " " Bum, bum, bum ! " Powerful speeches were made by the most learned of the kingdom. Foremost was Bishop Snowowl, who in a lengthy but profound speech clearly proved that the calamity had befallen the nation in consequence of the deep moral corruption of the people. This angel, he said, was removed by the Great Spirit, to prevent her being contaminated by their vices. She probably was now enjoying heavenly blessings in a purer and holier sphere, and only by constant fasting and praying could they hope to appease the wrath of the Divinity. " Moreover," he concluded, " it will be absolutely necessary to make large donations to the established church, and to give rich alms to the poor, if heaven is ever to be prevailed upon again to send this angel of peace into our midst. I shall move to lay the matter upon the table for the present, as I firmly believe that treasure and time expended in the recovery of Zuleika means throwing away time and treasure."

A heavy sigh of confession arose from the afflicted members of that exalted assembly. Soon after rose Noblefalcon. Combing his light moustaches with the long nails of his aristocratic claws, he replied as follows : "With due deference to your high virtues and deep wisdom, most illustrious Bishop, I venture to say that the great beauty and innocence of our deplored Zuleika have prompted some great villain to *steal* her from her parents and friends. I am so thoroughly convinced of this that I offer to start at once in search of our *protégée*, provided the venerable council will pass a resolution to reimburse me on my return for my eagerness, and to give me double the sum if I am successful. I am not asking the money for myself, but promise to divide it among my followers, whom I ask permission to choose from His Majesty's subjects."

"Well done, my dear Noblefalcon," exclaimed Armurat ; "and as an amendment, I, Armurat, Prince of India, promise to transfer the castle and domain of Falconburgh to you, Baron Noblefalcon, from the time of your return from such a hazardous undertaking; and I humbly ask that you choose me for one of your companions."

"Most willingly," rejoined the Falcon, "but with a

condition. As there cannot be two heads to one body, neither ought there to be two heads to an expedition. If you will be second to me in command, I shall rejoice to have you as my companion. But, my noble Prince "—and here the Falcon's look became very grave—" will you have the goodness to inform me what interest you take in this poor maiden's fate, that you are willing to risk life and fortune for one whom your human prejudices would forbid you to notice in your father's lofty halls ? "

Prince Armurat was mute with surprise at Noble-falcon's unexpected question, and before he could find a proper answer, the Falcon, seeing his embarrassment, continued as follows :

"With proper respect for your Royal Highness' rank and position, I prefer that Zulcika shall remain wherever she may be than that I should be instrumental in bringing her back to the beautiful valley to become—your prey." So speaking, he took his seat with a respectful bow toward the Prince. "Prey!" cried the Prince, starting from his seat. "Who dares to speak of her, the beautiful original of this picture, in such degrading words?" Taking the picture from the nutshell he kissed it, and, holding it high in the air, said in a loud and solemn voice : "Hear ye, all present, that

I promise and pledge my life to wed this maiden, lowly born as she may be, if ever I succeed in liberating her and safely conducting her to my father's castle."—"So be it!" sounded a response, unanimous, with the exception of Sir Chattering, who was distinctly heard to say, "provided she will have you." Nobody, however, took notice of this saucy remark.

The manly declaration made by the Prince satisfied the honest Falcon, and he shook hand and wing with the Prince in token of good fellowship. The council agreed to the reimbursement clause, with only one dissenting voice. The King promised to double the sum out of his private purse, and intrusted to Noblefalcon the sole command of the expedition.

That energetic nobleman proceeded with his arrangements forthwith.

Since Prince Armurat was to accompany him, Duke Shuhu's car was of course indispensable. The Duke made a long face, but dared not refuse.

Then the Falcon made out the list of his followers. First he put down the Aras, chief of the parrots, not for his intellectual qualities, for he did not believe they were very brilliant, but merely to give splendor to the cortége, and to impress the vulgar-minded, by whom outward show is generally regarded as true greatness, and who are easily awed by gaudy pageants. The second was a recluse owl, whose deep learning, profound insight in metaphysics, and clear understanding of the inherent laws of cause and effect had won for him high repute among the learned. Putting down number three of his choice, Noblefalcon addressed the King thus : " My Gracious Sovereign, ruler of the ancient Kingdom of Feathers, whose dominions extend as far as wings beat the winds, I must beseech you to send a messenger to His Majesty King Lion of the moors and forests, asking him to grant me as followers two of his subjects, whose accomplishments will be greatly needed to insure our success. Request of him his great jester, Monkey, manager of the Royal Theatre. His ever-ready wit and humorous manners make him a welcome companion, and he easily makes friends, and will thus obtain much useful information. I beseech you to ask also for the White Mouse, the chief engineer of the great King Lion, who is universally known for his deep studies in geology."

Of course King Eagle acceded to the Falcon's request, and soon the Ostrich, courier of the realm, was seen to leave the foreign office with despatches for King Lion. Being swift of foot, the Ostrich returned

the same evening with a courteous reply from King
Lion, sovereign of all the four-footers. He was only
too proud, he said, of lending some aid to so commend-
able an undertaking, He had commanded his high-
priest to order prayers to be said for the speedy recovery of their Fairy Queen. He had also sent his secretary with orders to the Camel to hold himself in readiness for departure, that he might convey the two
travellers to King Eagle's palace as soon as they should
be prepared to go. Towards noon of the same day
they arrived. The Mouse, white as snow, sat upon
the Camel's hump, clapping her tiny hands; while
Monkey, riding on the expressman's neck, amused
himself with making faces at the cheering crowd. For
these two travellers room had also to be made in Duke
Shuhu's aërial carriage. Noblefalcon's castle was
agreed upon as the place of meeting the next day,
when our travellers should be ready to start. The
castle was a primitive structure of granite, with little
embellishment and few comforts. Strength was the
sole purpose of its builder. It was placed upon a
solitary cliff. The stern Falcon would make no improvements or even repairs, and used to say, "From
my ancestors have I inherited this work. As it
was built by my first forefather so shall it be handed

down to my posterity. No improvements will I allow."

The King and his whole court had travelled over to Falconstone to lend prestige to the departing expedition. Bishop Snowowl spread his pinions, and invoked the celestial blessing upon them and their hazardous undertaking, although it had not his approval. When at last the foxes set off, flapping their leathery wing, the dense mass of spectators collected to see the knights-errant depart broke into the most vociferous hurrahs. When the cavalcade had been about half an hour on its way, Sir Chattering Magpie, all out of breath, alighted upon the Prince's shoulder, chattering vehemently, gesticulating with his wings and caressing the Prince's cheek with his left claw, until the latter got angry, and threatened to throw him out of the car. The pith of Magpie's chatter was to entreat the Prince, the preserver of his life, to permit him to join the expedition. When Armurat hesitated to allow him to accompany them, he threw himself on his tail, and begged and implored him to accept his services, insisting that without him he could never liberate Zuleika. Prince Armurat smiled, and considering his talent as a humorist, whose chatter might while away many tedious hours, he consented, when Sir Chatter-

ing, in the highest ecstasy, threw his wings around the
Prince's neck, and in an effort to kiss him bit his
cheek so that blood came.   Of course the Prince got
angry and Maggy was beside himself, but the Mouse
soon healed the slight wound.   The Prince gave a
stern lecture to Sir Chattering on account of general
indiscretion, adding, that if he betrayed one word of
their purpose to any stranger, he would cut off his
tongue without ceremony.   "Talkativeness," he concluded, " has defeated many a wise plan, and is fatal to
confidence and friendship."

I may, before I proceed further, give you the words
of the "mourners' song" with which the birds closed
the meeting which they held, when the news of the
abduction of Zuleika had reached them :—

SOLO.

Where is Zuleika,
  Rose of the meadow?
Gone is Zuleika,
  Lili's twin sister !

CHORUS.

Hark ye in the mountains !
  Hark ye in the prairies !
Hearken, ye thousands,
  Friends of our fairy !

SOLO.

Gone is Zuleika,
  Daisy's fair playmate ?—
Stolen is Zuleika,
  Pearl of the river !

CHORUS.

Hear ye in the mountains !
  Hear ye in the prairies !
Hear it, ye thousands,
  Friends of our fairy !

SOLO.

Stolen is Zuleika,
  Nymph of the river ?
Lost is Zuleika,
  Star of the heavens !

CHORUS.

Mourning in the mountains !
  Mourning in the prairies !
Mourn, all ye thousands,
  Friends of our fairy !

SOLO.

Up and down chasing !
  Hunt for the poacher !
Night and day watching !
  Down with the robber !

CHORUS.

Hunt through the mountains !
Hunt through the prairies !
Off with ye thousands !
Friends of our fairy !

CHAPTER III.

THE ABDUCTION OF ZULEIKA.

ZULEIKA went out one morning to play with the flowers on the river-bank. The fishes soon discovered that she was near, and gathered on the streamlet's border, splashing the crystal drops so that they fell like diamonds at her feet; they meant this as an invitation to come and play with them. No stronger persuasion was needed, and in a few minutes she was gambolling with her friends in the clear water. Tingle, tingle, tingle, sounded the warning bell in the midst of all this fun. Like lightning Zuleika leaped on shore to put her dress on, and hardly had she done so when a great noise arose, increasing to the roar of a hurricane; the poor girl became so frightened at what she saw and heard that she sank down in the grass, powerless to move. The bravest boy would have taken to his heels had he seen what she saw. Just imagine: two huge dragons came flying

3*

through the air; they snorted as if a hundred steam-
engines were all starting at once, and from their cop-
pery nostrils issued streams of living fire; and behind
them they drew a golden carriage, covered with precious stones. The wheels of the carriage threw off
sparks of fire, and looked like the spinning wheels
which we admire so much in fireworks. The carriage
was occupied by two hideous-looking men, one very
old, the other in his prime. The dragons and their
carriage alighted on the lawn, a short distance from
Zuleika. The strangers instantly alighted and came
towards where she sat. At this moment the bell was
tingling so loud that even these rough men heard it.

"Do not be frightened, my sugar-plum," said the old
man; "do not be afraid of us; we are not come to harm
you, my dove. On the contrary, I intend to confer
upon you the greatest blessing that ever could fall to
woman's lot; I come to make you the daughter of the
great Zamurungi, whom vulgar-minded people call the
magician of the north pole. There is no maiden in
Asia worthy to become the wife of this noble youth,
my son (who stood closely by, grinning) but Zuleika,
the fairest flower of the secluded valley. Come, then,
my lily, come into our carriage, and we will at once
drive to our splendid palace in Siberia, to celebrate

your wedding, which shall be more than royal; it will be supernaturally grand! Come." At the touch of his hand a chill ran throughout Zuleika's body, everything began spinning and whirling around and before her, she uttered a cry of anguish, and fell upon the grass, senseless. Her father, hearing the cry, appeared on the spot at the moment the strangers were lifting her into the carriage; he sprang upon the old man, but a touch of his hand threw old father Pan prostrate. The fall stunned him, and when he came to his senses again, all was quiet and nothing to be seen. He took it all for an ugly dream, but when Zuleika did not return the reality became unquestionable.

It is a time-honored custom to introduce fresh personages to the reader as they make their appearance in a story, and thus remove all doubt of their identity should they ever meet again in some other book. The old man who has just taken Zuleika away is Zamurungi the Great, as he calls himself, magician from the north pole. He is of athletic constitution and choleric temperament. He has a hooked nose with a jerk at the end, caused by a cherry-like lump, a comfortable saddle for any little teasing imp that would dare to mount it. His piercing eyes were deep set, and his bushy eyebrows so overhanging that the eyes looked like coals behind a grating; on his bumpy head grew hair as thick as porcupine quills. His clothes were decidedly not made in Broadway; he had his own tailor. His pants were made of rhinoceros skin, his jacket was cut from the hide of some antediluvian saurus, his boots were made of horse-hoofs, richly inlaid with gold and diamonds. The other is the wizard's son—a rather insignificant youth, of lymphatic constitution, melancho-choleric temperament, and a face in which there is malice enough to show that he may commit any act of cruelty and consider it pastime. He assumed airs which made him look like a wizard dandy. His upper lip took great pains to raise a moustache, but the hairs were so coarse and far between that it resembled the whiskers on a cat's nose. His chin paraded a goat's beard, only not so rich. His nose was a decided snub, and his eyes fishy. He wore rattlesnake gloves, boa-constrictor jacket, salamander shoes, and a toad-skin cap.

The two old people of the secluded valley were in utter despair. Mrs. Pan assures her husband that this will kill her, and she sits down weeping, expecting death to come and take her at any moment; but every morning her husband lays fresh and delicious fruit at her side, the choicest he can find, and thus she remains alive. He, poor creature, can find no tears to relieve his grief. He wanders about from place to place where they had walked together, stopping at every place where they had worked together, planting flowers and making bowers, here laying out pathways and there forming archways through the woods. There was her bathing-place, and in this shade she loved to lie down and sleep. Where was his darling now? To him nature had lost her charms; over her rosy tints a black veil was drawn, and the birds sang sadly. Every morning at sunrise he found tears hanging on the flowers; they wept for Zuleika. In the evening he sat in front of the hut, listening to the whispers of the wind. No doubt they knew all about his darling, but he did not understand their language. When the birds were talking together he often heard the name of his Zuleika. The swallows, in particular, mentioned her very often.

Noblefalcon had directed Horseshoenose to drive first to the hermitage in the secluded valley; and not a little alarmed were our two simple people at the sight of that remarkable expedition. Mrs. Pan said that now death had come for her, and she fell on her knees to sue for mercy; for although she had often wished to die, she now discovered that life was dear, and it took

some time before Prince Armurat could convince her
that he was not Death. But as soon as she heard that
he and his companions had set out to recover their
lamented daughter, she forgot death and her fears,
cried and laughed alternately, embraced now the
Prince, then her husband, and took the Falcon by the
wing to dance with him ; but this grave personage drew
back his wing : he never danced. Monkey enjoyed the
fun better, and was soon on top of her head by means
of her long braids. But when he became thus imper-
tinent the Falcon called him to order.

Noblefalcon had hoped to get information regarding
Zuleika's abduction, but all Mr. Pan knew about it
was, that two men carried her off in a carriage drawn
by dragons. At this moment Sir Chattering, who had
been off to gossip with the birds in the neighborhood,
returned in company with a red sparrow, who, he said,
had witnessed the whole scene from beginning to end.
Here is the red sparrow's account : " My Lord Noblefalcon, I was quietly hatching my eggs in the reeds,
when I saw Zuleika stepping into the river to bathe,
and I thought of the time when my young ones would
leave their shells and our fairy queen would come to
play with them, when suddenly two huge monsters
came snorting through the air and alighted with a car

close by me. Two men jumped out and put our beloved Zuleika in that car, and then hurried off. I
heard the old man say that he was Zamurungi, and
that they were driving to his palace in Siberia." The
sparrow, being a very talkative bird, had a great deal
more to say.

"Then we have to encounter a powerful enemy, and
our task will be difficult beyond measure," said the
Baron, walking gravely up and down with folded
wings. "Now it occurs to me that my father, in his
travels through Asia, stayed a while at the castle of
Earl Griffin, one of the wizard's subjects, and dreadful
stories did he tell of the wickedness of the old sinner.
It will be best for us first to visit Earl Griffin, and see
whether we can profit by this circumstance."

Wise people have said that small causes often contain the germs of great effects, although they may lie
dormant in the shell for years and years. Perhaps our
travellers are on the eve of discovering the truth of
this saying. Fortunately, Noblefalcon's father had
been a learned man, and had drawn a careful map of
all his travels, from which his son distinctly remembered the situation of the Earl's castle; and thither he
drove his foxes.

Had potted ham or condensed milk been prepared

at that remote time, how easy would have been their
journey! But as it was, the difficulty of finding pro-
visions for themselves and team in the wilderness
through which they had to travel was great indeed,
but as many of our explorers know how to surmount
incredible obstacles by energy and will, so did these
travellers also, and they were rewarded for their perseverance by reaching Castle Griffinstone on the eve of
the thirty-third day of their exhausting journey.

CHAPTER IV.

CASTLE GRIFFINSTONE.

HEERED by the sight of the castle, the hungry foxes made one more desperate effort, and descended slowly with their burden in front of the huge portals. Two gigantic shaggy wolverines, concealed in their burrows, kept watch, and suddenly leaping forward would have devoured the poor foxes in an instant, had not Prince Armurat jumped from the car, and, brandishing his sword, commanded them to stand aside. Disappearing in their caves, they turned like spinning-tops, peeped out again, and gave a howl that made the poor monkey creep under the seat in a twinkle. This noise awoke a strange, hideous-looking creature, so grotesque in shape that it would have puzzled our naturalists to determine whether it was fish, bird, or reptile. Two long jaws came poking out of one of the loopholes of the tower, opening so wide that a six-feet rod might have been put between them without touching; and the creatures roared out to know who the rabble were that so disturbed the quiet of Lord Griffin's castle.

"Good friends and knights-errant on their travels through Asia," answered the Falcon. "Come, good porter, let us in. Don't you remember my father, Baron Falcon, from King Eagle's empire? He was a great friend of Earl Griffin."—"By the little toe of Zamurungi the Great," cried the porter, in his croaking voice, "are you the son of that merry nobleman, who passed a whole winter with my master, and amused him so much with his funny stories? What a pity that Earl Griffin is not at home; but he will return to-morrow; meanwhile come in, and make yourself comfortable, and be merry as your father was." With this he withdrew his jaws, and came scrambling down the stairs as fast as his clumsy and time-worn limbs would let him. Soon after the keys turned in the rusty locks with a shriek, the bolts gave way with a growl, the hinges creaked, and the doors flew back.

The whole castle yard seemed suddenly alive. Grooms came running to attend the flying foxes, and footmen conducted Mouse, Owl, Monkey, and Parrot through the kitchen into a warm apartment on the ground-floor. The Aras turned up his nose in disdain, plumed his feathers, and appeared to take great offence at the familiar tone of the servants. They, however, took no notice of it. When, however, some delicious fruit and wine were brought in, he turned his nose down again, took his seat at the table, and commenced eating and drinking, mumbling, "The wise make a law of necessity." The steward, too, would not permit Magpie to enter the drawing-room, insisting that his place was down stairs, where his comrades had already made themselves comfortable. But he grew saucy, and told them to mind their business; that he was Sir Chattering Magpie, and a volunteer; no hireling, but a gentleman, also a friend of the Prince; and continued chattering in such an unbroken strain of disconnected sentences, that he so completely bewildered the not over-smart steward, that he allowed him to enter with a most courteous bow.

"How lucky it is," said Noblefalcon, after he and the Prince had finished their dinner and sat smoking a kind of narcotic weed; "how lucky for us that Earl Griffin will not return until to-morrow; this will give our friends time and opportunity to find out all they possibly can about the wizard and his palace." Sir

Chattering was sent down to the four companions on the ground-floor, with instructions to use all their ingenuity. The Falcon reminded Maggy to be on his guard, and not betray a syllable of their real purpose; and assured the gossip with a solemn oath, that if he did so he would forever leave him in those icy regions. The poor Magpie shivered, for he knew that Noble-falcon was always as good as his word.

Later in the evening, while yet laying plans, they were startled by the Owl's frantic hootings; he came hobbling into the room, rubbing his eyes with the knuckles of his wings, and hooted that he was going blind, and should never more see the moon. Noble-falcon jumped from his seat, and begged him to explain the matter more clearly. " O my lord, my lord, we are all lost, lost forever ; the heavens are on fire, and the earth begins to burn." It was clear that something very unusual had taken place, else the Owl, usually so self-possessed, would not have lost all balance of mind. Therefore the two leaders rushed out on the battlements. There they found their followers all assembled ; and a wonderful sight was before them. Half the sky appeared all in a blaze ! Long fiery flashes issued like rockets from the northern horizon, and joining in a point right over head formed a gigantic palm-leaf.

Soon they scattered and spread into a thousand independent flames in all directions like sky-rockets. Suddenly they all were concentrated at one spot, forming a crimson disk, bordered by zigzag lines of the prismatic colors. Then when scarcely formed they broke up, to assemble in another place. These changes occurred so rapidly, and new combinations were formed so quickly, that it was hard to keep track of them. Soon, to the amazement of all observers, a rolling mass, like illuminated mist of a summer morning, rose from the horizon ; it was preceded by a quivering yellow light, and soon covered the already brilliant sky. Over this volleys of color and light would again be poured from a masked battery below the horizon. In short, there seemed to be a monster conflagration in the sky, and the earth appeared in jeopardy. All stood trembling. What could it mean ?

"If only Bishop Snowowl were here," cried the Parrot, his many-colored feathers shaking like the rays in the sky. " I am sure this is the beginning of doomsday, and we shall all be ushered into the other world along with the rabble here, without confession and absolution, with all our sins on our backs. Mercy ! O mercy ! To leave this world at a moment when all the pale girls of this land are madly in love with me, is heartbreaking.

Let us fly, my lord, while we yet may ; I will go and have the car ready at once." And the poor Parrot started to bring the foxes before the car. "Stop, fool, and await the orders of your superiors !" The Owl uttered not a word, but sat steadily staring in the ocean of glaring light. He was sure it would blind him, but it was so splendid to look at, and well worth the risk ! The Monkey had been taking too freely of burning ice-water to mind anything ; it had set his brains on fire and he was not astonished at anything. Things without sympathized with his fancies within. Maggy would have crept into the Prince's coat pocket, but for the fear of breaking the feathers of his beautiful tail. The little Mouse alone showed no signs of consternation ; he too looked at it, but with sheer delight. He had repeatedly attempted to attract the Prince's or Noble-falcon's attention, but without success. The Monkey's capers at last aroused the Prince from his deep contemplation, and then he heard his name called ; but very faintly, for it was only with a squeak of a mouse. "Is it you, Dory ?" said the Prince ; "what do you want ?" and he beckoned the little creature to come near to his ear. The little white Mouse scrambled to the top of his shoulder, and then carefully descending, perched himself upon Armurat's forefinger. " By the peculiar

twinkle in your rosy eyes, I presume you have some
news to tell me ; let us step aside that I may be better
able to hear you," said the Prince, seating himself on
the further side of the battlements, apart from the rest
of the company.

"Do not be afraid, dear Prince," began little Dory,
carefully arranging his long thin moustaches, with a
feeling of great consequence ; "do not be frightened,
for the apparition in the heavens is nothing but a great
display of fireworks, got up by the wizard Zamurungi,
to amuse the interesting young lady whom he—"

"By the head of my fathers, what do you mean ?"
cried the Prince, with a violent shudder, which would
have thrown him over the battlement, had not Dory
perceived it in time, and with extraordinary presence
of mind swung his body from Armurat's finger on to
the toe of his shoe, thus restoring his equilibrium, else
he must have been precipitated in the gushing stream
below. In justice to Dory I must here remark, that
the Prince in his excitement did not notice this great
service, and the mouse was too noble-hearted ever to
allude to it or claim a reward ; the consciousness of
having saved the Prince's life was compensation enough
for him. And we should never have heard of it, had
not luckily the Owl for once jerked his eyes from the

cordially hated flames towards the spot where they both sat, and which incident was after his death found mentioned in his autobiography.

"Is this the way you reward your faithful friends, to fling them into the river? Is this the price for all the trouble I have taken to find out all I could to further the object of this expedition?" piped the little thing; and his nose pouted as much as to say, "Henceforth I keep my mouth shut."

"Forgive me, my dear little pet," replied the Prince, stroking his white fur affectionately; "I could not help it, you took me so by surprise; I did not know that you had already set to work; don't be angry, but go on telling me all you know."

"Perhaps it was my own fault. I ought not to commence with the end instead of the beginning, and I will correct my error by starting from the proper point. While Monkey was sipping his spiced ice-water, and Owl rehearsing the materials for his future memoirs, as he said, and while Parrot was flirting with the kitchen girls, I stole quietly away, without being perceived by the servants. I was very curious to inspect these interesting piles of stone, heaped together in the early days of creation (for in a remote corner of one of the dark murky vaults was deeply carved: Anno I.).

I went on to explore further, and found this to be the most remarkable piece of architecture I ever saw. If it be true that architecture is the real exponent of a people's character, then this must have been built before law and order appeared in the world. But what an infamous place this is!"

" Infamous place? Why, Dory?"

" Hush, hush. I have not come to that part yet; you know I have to be cautious with you, lest you go into a fit again. Were I to tell you at once all the horrors that I have seen and heard in this castle, we would both be in the river in the next minute; therefore patience, my friend."

" Nonsense, you little torment; but how could you see so many horrible things in so short a time?"

" I believe, Prince, as distances are greater to mice than men, time must also be longer with us.

" But, having explored the superstructure of the palace, I descended to the infra-terrestrial region of this gigantic pile of stone, where I found enormous cellars, filled with treasures of all sorts and descriptions, heaped together without method or purpose, seemingly piled up to fill the owner's heart with the selfish and cold delight of possession only, coupled with a feeling of constant fear of losing them. I was descending

4

deeper and deeper into the bowels of this gigantic warehouse, when I thought that I heard a distant moaning. I followed the direction of that sound, which increased in distinctness as I advanced. Presently I came to a door, behind which I heard the woful groaning of a human voice. I tried to force an entrance, but there was nothing my teeth could lay hold of. Impenetrative stone and metal rendered all my efforts fruitless. At last I discovered a small hole under the ceiling right over the door, probably serving as means for ventilation. With a desperate leap I found myself in the apartment. By means of a large carbuncle in the centre of the roof, I saw a poor woman prostrate on the earth, scratching the hard stones, as if she wanted to dig herself out. She presented as pitiful a sight as I ever saw. She accompanied her operation with a mournful song, which made me cry hot tears. She was insane. She must have been beautiful before she was incarcerated here. She was black as ebony. Not being able to help her, I went on my errand of discovery. I perceived a similar hole in the wall opposite to the one I had entered. In less than a second I found myself in another cell, occupied by an equally unfortunate being. She was of a yellow color, and sat lamenting on a stone. She must have been some princess, because in one corner I saw a broken crown of pure gold and pearls. Her language I did not understand ; she must have been born in a very distant country.

"Adjoining this cell was another prison, which I entered in the same way as the former two. Here a nut-brown and haggard beauty was imprisoned. In this manner I went from cell to cell, and each one contained a wretched woman. I tried to attract the attention of some of them, but in vain ; they did not heed me. Dungeon joined on dungeon, and misery on misery ; and when I had passed through 199 and entered the last, I found in it a beautiful fair girl, who had evidently been there but a few days. Keep quiet, my prince, or I must break off in my narrative. The battlement is high and the river deep. She was seated upon a coarse granite block, her elbow rested upon a square stone at her side. She was weeping bitterly when I entered ; but after a while she lifted her head, dried her tears, and seizing a musical instrument resembling our Southern mandolines, she commenced singing one of the saddest songs that I ever heard. Feeling a great interest in this unhappy being, I jumped down and climbed noiselessly upon the top of the stone at her side. She looked most beautiful, with her

large black eyes filled with tears, as I gazed into
them."

"But, Dory, tell me, is she Zuleika, the idol of my
soul? Tell me—have pity on me!" cried Armurat,
unable to restrain himself any longer.

"Patience, patience, Royal Highness; all will be re-
vealed to you in the proper course. When she had
finished her mournful ditty I gave her a slight pinch,
at which she jumped up, screaming fearfully. Catching
sight of me, she ordered me to go away; but to go
away was not in my plan, therefore I sat still. Here
I must pause to make a brief remark.

"Is it not a great pity that your race, my Prince,
and mine live in perpetual warfare? Your race is un-
questionably the stronger, but mine is the subtler;
your race will never conquer mine, assuredly mine can
never subdue yours · neither is it our desire to do so.
Believe me, we are passionately fond of mankind, and
are most happy in man's neighborhood. It is a well-
known fact that we follow in man's track, like his dog
or cat. We should never think of harming you were
we not goaded to it in retaliation for acts of cruelty
and murder."

"Hum, hum; I never thought you could plead a
case so well, my little rogue; one would think you had

studied jurisprudence at our university, and learned how to invert the actual state of things completely," replied Armurat. "The real truth of the matter is, that the pilfering propensity of your tribe is so great, that you would even steal the food from the very mouth of our children, were you permitted to have your own way."

"Ah! the dear children," resumed Dory; "on their part I grieve most over the unhappy state of affairs in our social intercourse with men. Think what happy days your boys and girls could enjoy with ours, were the times such as to permit a friendly communion; and believe me your little folks would profit greatly by it."

"And may I ask my attorney-general what talents you possess and propose to teach our children? Is it the cultivated art of pilfering?" asked Prince Armurat, pulling Dory's long moustaches.

"I will bite you if you do that again," said Dory, hurt by the Prince's indelicate allusion to the ignoble propensity of his race. "As to pilfering, as you choose to term the desire to procure our daily bread, your boys and girls are too far advanced in that branch of the fine arts to need any instruction."

"Come, Dory, explain in what the advantages consist."

"No, I won't tell them now, because you are so conceited, and only wish to amuse yourself at my expense."

"Earnestly, Dory, in what do you think we can profit by your society?"

"Probably you will call it boasting and bragging; but I assure you that all created beings, not merely man and mouse, can learn from one another. Unfortunately, every one of us is so self-satisfied and prejudiced, that he thinks he is wiser than the rest, and as his father and grandfathers did things they ought to be done. Now, observing and comparing things that come in my way, I find that in a measure as any being overcomes his innate predilections, and adopts superior qualities possessed by others, he rises in knowledge, consequently power, above the rest. Your race has adopted this course already to a great extent, and that accounts for your superiority; but still greater will you become as soon as you advance further in the same direction, and watch your fellow-creatures still more closely—above all, with more feeling of friendship and sympathy. Lay aside your insolent pride with which you look down upon us who habitually, and for comfort's sake, walk upon four or six legs."

"Why don't you follow our example yourself, and

overcome that antiquated prejudice of walking on four legs ? "

" There is a good reason for asking that question. I myself have formed a society in King Lion's woodlands, called the ' Society of the Two-legged Movement,' and I expect great results from it, though I know from my own experience that it takes many generations to overcome a deep-rooted prejudice. Your people have very wisely imitated the birds in the walk upon two legs, which leaves your hands free for other purposes."

" But, my learned professor, you might out of courtesy give us the credit of having ourselves invented the art of walking erect."

" Not so, Royal Highness, which I would clearly prove had I my collected notes here ; not so, the birds did it for you. You have learned most things from our fellow-creatures ; your only merit is having sense enough to appropriate all the different talents which they separately possess. There is cousin Beaver ; from him you learned how to build a house ; the Frog taught you how to swim gracefully, while the Tailor-bird showed you how to sew your clothes ; the bees and ants taught you the blessings of industry (which, by the way, you have learned from us ; but I pass that over).

Imitating the foxes, you dug your cellars and built your vaults ; the Pelican taught you the art of fishing, and the Lion how to hunt ; the shell-fish instructed you in ornamental architecture, the sword-fish gave you an idea how to make your weapons ; and—"

" Enough, enough, you insolent wretch. By and by you will say the gluttons taught us how to eat, the sloth happiness in idleness, and the unmentionable animals how to wallow in the mire. Owing to your nonsense we have almost forgotten the young lady in that horrid dungeon. Be quick, and say what you found out."

" Promise first, Prince, to grant a treaty of peace between our people as soon as you become King."

" Hush, hush, my arch diplomat ; leave this matter until that, I hope, distant day shall arrive ; not a word more about it now."

By the Prince's earnest tone Dory saw that he had to abandon his scheme for the present. He felt mortified that his efforts to raise the social position of his race in Armurat's future dominion had failed. With an effort he overcame his desire of revenging himself by keeping silent, and he continued to relate the result of his investigations.

" I had to do something to attract the lady's attention, and took refuge in mimicking. I succeeded ; she became interested, and finally broke out into a hearty laugh. She held her beautiful finger out to me, but withdrew it, terribly frightened, when I kissed it. By and by she grew bolder, took me in her hand, caressed and, will you believe it, finally kissed me, and it is not vanity to confess, that this was the swiftest and most complete victory I have made in all my life. I spoke to her, but, alas! she did not understand our language —a provoking defect in her education. She laughed at my most serious speeches, as if I had said the drollest things. Then I bethought myself of a pantomime, fell on my knees, put my right hand upon my heart, stretched forth my left towards her—just as I have seen you human lovers do, when you pop the question—and then squeaked as pitifully as I could. This had the desired effect; she took me again in her hand, stroked and kissed me, crying, ' Hush, hush, thou droll thing ; thou breakest my heart ;' and now tears came gushing from her eyes, ran down her pale cheeks, and nearly drowned me. ' Just so, just so,' she continued, ' did Prince Amadelulu kneel before me, while he swore eternal love and devotion. O my beloved one, where are you now ? I know you hunt all over the sandy desert, you will ascend the lofty mountains and search every valley, but you will not find your—Fatima!' "

"Not Zuleika," exclaimed the Prince, "thanked be the gods!"

"Only Fatima," said Dory, dryly.

"Go on," said the Prince.

"'Woe, woe is me, who in the pride of my heart sent you to the top of the cliff to get me the beautiful flower which only grows upon that inaccessible rock. When you had culled the flower, and came to offer it to me as a token of your love, I was gone—gone for-ever!'

"Here her feelings overcame her; she dropped her arms, so that I fell to the floor, and wept bitterly. Here was a new perplexity. I was determined to learn more, but how induce her to speak again? I once more climbed the stone table, assumed a frantic attitude, and screamed as loudly as I could. With the greatest effort I succeeded in attracting her attention again, and the moment she looked at me I pulled my whiskers, and tore the hair from my head, and so on.

"'Good Spirits! dost thou understand me, Mouse?' she cried. 'So did Amadelulu tear his hair and cry in agony and despair when he found I was gone. A thousand curses upon the head of the villain Zamurungi.' Here I nodded my head and clapped my hands in token of applause. 'He really understands

me,' she said; 'are you a prince whom that demon
has changed to a mouse?' I shook my head deliberately, having no desire to be taken for so exalted a
personage. 'No? what then are you?'

"'Only an humble mouse, desirous to help you out of
your misery,' said I, speaking slowly and with great
emphasis, as one must always do when speaking to
foreigners; but it was useless: she did not comprehend
me. Afraid that she would remain silent, I commenced
blowing kisses at her. But my apprehensions proved
groundless, for her desire to speak was aroused, and
quite as great as mine was to listen; and she told me
how she was stolen away by Zamurungi, and carried to
his summer palace, about one hundred miles from here,
to the north. Both villains, she said, were continually
persecuting her with offers of marriage—the old man
for the young, and the young for himself. 'But, O
Amadelulu! how could I forget you?' At this moment
the keeper appeared with some food, which compelled
me to hide in the ventilator. Peeping over the edge
as much as I dared, I heard the keeper say, 'The great
wizard gives a brilliant entertainment to-night for his
beautiful new bride; all the sky is in a blaze right over
his palace. This display of fireworks would have been
given in your honor, had you not foolishly rejected the

offers of the great Zamurungi's son.' Being anxious to report to you I hastened away, and entered at the moment when Owley's lamentations caused you to rush on the battlements. Behold, it is a marvellous sight!"

When the Mouse had finished, Armurat called the Falcon and explained to him the nature of the phenomenon; they heartily laughed at their absurd fears caused by the fireworks, but were horrified by the Mouse's report. After some meditation, the Falcon said,

"Now, Prince, you must write a few lines to the ill-fated Fatima, entreating her to relate everything she knows of the wizard, his palace, and Zuleika, to the Mouse; and mention to her that restoration to liberty and union with her lover depend upon the success of a plan which she can further by giving the desired information. Let the Mouse carry this to her instantly. Upon her answer, in a measure, our future arrangements depend."

Armurat proceeded at once to Griffin's study, and taking a piece of lotus-leaf, wrote as follows:—

"FAIR LADY,—My little page, Dory, has related to me his interview with you. He understands your language, though you do not understand his. I deeply deplore your situation, and I hope, at a not distant day, to restore you to your parents. All will depend upon our success in subduing our common foe, the wizard Zamurungi. Pray relate to the messenger all that you know about the magician, his palace, and Zuleika, his last prey.

"A SYMPATHIZING FRIEND.

" P. S.—The strictest secrecy is enjoined on all engaged in this perilous undertaking. I have therefore given orders to Dory to destroy this leaf."

It was past midnight. Every one except the guards had gone to bed, and Dory found no difficulty in reaching Fatima's cell unobserved. The poor girl had wept herself to sleep. The little Mouse crept stealthily up to her face, and stroking her velvet cheek with his little tongue, gave her a slight pinch with his fore feet. Exclaiming, "O my Amadelulu!" Fatima awoke. At the sight of the little four-footer, who had quickly jumped upon her finger, presenting the lotus-leaf, she trembled and screamed; but soon recognizing her little friend of a few hours ago, she became calm, and began caressing him; but he suddenly disappeared in the folds of her dress when he heard the guard open the door, and with a growl ask the cause of her screams.

"My good keeper," cried Fatima, with great presence of mind, "I am so glad that I am awake, and again hear your familiar voice. I had such a fearful dream : a monster dragon came slowly creeping up to me ; it had seven heads, and every head wanted to kiss me. I tremble yet. Did you ever dream of being pursued, good keeper?"

"There's no one dares to pursue me, even in a dream," hissed the herculean keeper, "and I advise you to keep awake rather than indulge in such luxuries as dreams ;" and bang slammed the door.

The lines upon the lotus-leaf were so many rays of light thrown into Fatima's prison of despair. She could hardly realize the fact that she was once more in communication with the outer world. Little Dory was almost smothered with kisses, but knowing how anxiously his return was looked for, he tried every possible means for inducing her to give the much-desired information. But Fatima, completely absorbed in contemplating the note so strangely delivered, had entirely forgotten what her friend asked her to do; and having carefully put the lotus-leaf in her bosom, she was soon lost in revery, probably picturing to herself the reunion with her Amadelulu. What was to be done ? Dory knew well enough that young maidens, when dreaming of their lovers, are immensely busy for hours within themselves, yet idle concerning the rest of the world.

"I must be bold, and do a desperate thing, even at the risk of my life," piped the little thief; whereupon he dived like lightning into Fatima's bosom, caught the lotus-leaf, and ran off with it before she had time to crush him in her justifiable wrath. The next moment Fatima perceived the nimble creature looking down from the hole under the ceiling, holding the lotus-leaf in his outstretched paw, pointing to the writing with the other. This brought the unfortunate girl's mind back to her hopeless situation. With tears in her eyes she implored the little Mouse to come down again, but he shook his head mischievously. Fatima felt keenly that he was the only hope in her desperate plight, and therefore implored him with every name of endearment to descend, promising to relate all she knew. Although this was exactly what he wanted, the scamp took delight in teasing her a while, by coming down a short distance and then suddenly disappearing in the ventilator, leaving Fatima in despair lest he had gone altogether; and then presently his little eyes and nose would peep over the edge, and he would look at her with an artful chuckle.

At last, with great dexterity he jumped upon the agitated girl's hand, who immediately began thus :

"Difficult beyond conception will be the attempt of my sympathizing friend and his followers to recover the lady he calls by the sweet name of Zuleika. Tender and sensitive indeed she appeared to be when she entered the palace, at the same time the Griffin came to carry me hither. That palace no woman ever left, save to be buried in these awful dungeons. Of Zuleika I know nothing more. I was told that the wizard always has a new building erected for the special use of a 'new bride,' as the vulgar people used to call us there. Zamurungi is one of the most powerful of his diabolic tribe ; and all that I know of him concerning his power and weakness is, that he can only be defeated by the interposition of a good spirit, who is mightier than himself. With this spirit of virtue he carried on a war of life and death for ages, and at last, not by power, but by an artful stratagem, he succeeded in shutting up his adversary in a heart made of ebony painted white ; its destruction alone can liberate the Good Spirit. Where it is hidden I know not, but this much I have heard, that it is enclosed in an ironwood chest, placed deep in some cavern under the palace. moreover, this chest is watched by a monster more

hideous than either you or I can imagine. He has
three times nine heads, with three times nine eyes.
Forth from his nostrils, in each head, does he pour
liquid streams of fire at every breath ; an adamantine
horn, pointed as a needle, ornaments each nose ; huge
teeth, harder than flint, protrude from the upper jaws.

"This monster is the eldest son of Zamurungi by his
first wife, the daughter of Chaos. No power on earth
can defeat this monster ; and while he lives the liberation of the Good Spirit is impossible, and until that
is effected Zamurungi is invulnerable. The castle is
not hard to find ; it rears its turrets proudly in the sky ;
it stands due north from here ; it was built shortly
after the imprisonment of the Good Spirit, and is the
favorite residence of the old wizard. It is constructed
entirely of crystallized tears, wrung in sorrow and
agony from men, beasts, and birds. Alas! that it
should be true—tears that we wretched women shed
within these gloomy walls are ingeniously preserved
as material for current repairs.

"This, my little messenger, is all the information I
can give you. Go tell it to my kind friend ; but, my dear
little Mouse, come and see me once more ere you leave
for the magician's palace." Kissing the white Mouse
affectionately she put him on the floor, and he bounded

off through the well-known channel. In the eagerness to relate and listen, they both had forgotten the
lotus-leaf; it had slipped out of Fatima's hand, and
fallen behind the stone.

Falcon and the Prince had been up all night, waiting
for Dóry's return. It was now almost daylight, when
patter patter his little feet hurried over the floor.

Noblefalcon met him half way, seized him with his
long-nailed claw, and put him on the table; but he
instantly jumped down upon Armurat's hand and commenced smoothing his skin, sadly ruffled by the Falcon's handling. When after the elapse of some minutes the Mouse made no preparation to begin his report, Armurat impatiently said :—

"Please, Dory, make your toilet at a later hour; we
do not stand upon ceremony."

But he did not suffer himself to be interrupted, and
smoothed away, licking and stroking his skin until
every shining hair lay in its proper place. This accomplished, he said :—

"Bad news, bad news, my lords! Better for us to put
our heads again in Duke Shuhu's carriage, than thrust
them into the jaws of a monster with three times nine
heads, three times nine eyes, with adamantine daggers
upon his noses, and flint swords in each jaw;" thus con-

tinuing until he had related everything Fatima had said.

After the receipt of this discouraging news Dory was sent to call the whole company together for a grand council.

At this juncture the whole enterprise was near coming to grief by a disagreement between the Prince and Falcon. Prince Armurat, in the ardor of his youthful love, wanted to set off immediately; he insisted upon finding and fighting the monster at once, in spite of his eyes, heads, daggers, swords, and streams of fire. But Noblefalcon said "No," most decidedly. His plan was, that the Parrot, Owl, and Mouse should precede them; the Parrot as herald to announce their intended visit, but the Owl and Mouse should quietly slip into the palace at night; the latter might travel on Owl's back. Prince Armurat pronounced this a most shameful and cowardly plan, unworthy of a man, and declared he would never give his consent.

"Remember, Prince," said the Falcon, deliberately, —"remember the condition your Royal Highness pledged yourself to fulfil before we started from King Eagle's palace."

Exalted personages do not easily brook contradiction; still less do they like to be reminded of inconvenient promises. Stamping his foot on the floor, he exclaimed, "But I will have it so, and will hear no more contradictions."

"Very well, then I will return with my foxes and report myself to King Eagle, who intrusted this expedition to me *solely*," replied the immovable Falcon.

At this moment Maggy came in. Judging in what state affairs were, he perched himself on the back of a chair, and began chattering, "Vanity, haughtiness—haughtiness, vanity—vanity, haughtiness—haughtiness, vanity."

"Your fooling is ill-timed," interrupted Noblefalcon in a harsh voice ; "hence, and prepare for our immediate departure to King Eagle's court."

"I am a volunteer, and may do as I like," replied Maggy, saucy as ever. "Why is my austere Baron so angry with me ? I was only repeating two new words which I have learned this moment ; this is my custom, any way, of committing to memory anything I wish to retain. I am about laying in a stock of knowledge."

Luckily for Sir Chattering, the Owl came in at this moment and diverted Sir Falcon's wrath. Both parties laid their plans before him, asking his opinion.

"I intend to give no offence," said Owl, "but my opinion is that Noblefalcon's plan is by far the most sensible of the two, even if giving but little hope of success; while yours, my Prince, begging a thousand pardons, is a madman's, without method."

In most cases when two are quarrelling, and call a third for a decision, the umpire makes an enemy of him that he puts on the wrong side, and a friend of the opponent; and neutrality makes enemies of both parties. But if a third and fourth person side with the umpire in his decision, the one in the wrong gradually yields, and an agreement is effected.

The Prince gave a savage look at the Owl, but when Maggy came to his comrade's support, and when the Parrot, who had stepped in by this time, also agreed with Falcon, he gradually assented to the Baron's plan.

With customary promptness and precision, this true hero proceeded to make the proper arrangements forthwith.

"You, Aras," he said, "hold yourself in readiness to depart within half an hour for Zamurungi's castle. Being our herald, you are to announce to this mighty potentate our intended visit to his court. Tell him that we shall arrive there by to-morrow night, subject, of course, to Earl Griffin's return."

The Aras looked discomforted at this peremptory

command to start and leave his many interesting in-
trigues, and when the Falcon added : " You shall not
go alone ; Owl and Mouse will accompany you ;" he
burst out,

" Pretty company, pretty company !" only by way of
giving vent to his anger, and not to disparage his comrades.

As soon as the three scouts had started, the two no-
blemen went to sleep, utterly exhausted by the many
exciting occurrences of the night.

CHAPTER V.

ZAMURUNGI'S SUMMER PALACE.

BOUT four in the afternoon of the following day, our travellers arrived in sight of the
mighty palace, which had almost the look
of a whole city, so extensive was it. Owl and Mouse
fell back, according to orders. Aras alone proceeded,
feeling anything but cheerful.

Arriving at the grotesque portals, he was met by a
howl from two immense white polar bears ; these the
Parrot did not mind much, but the two harpy-like monsters at the top of each turret, eying him so tenderly,
made the blood rush to his heart.

"What do you want ?" roared a quartet from these
watchmen and women. Every feather of our dandy
stood on end.

"I am the herald of His Royal Highness Prince
Armurat, and Baron Noblefalcon, sent to announce

their speedy arrival at this palace ; they are desirous
of doing homage to His Illustrious Majesty Zamurungi,
of world-wide fame," stammered Aras.

One of the pages, who seemed entirely made up of
knots and sticks, shot off into the palace, and was back
again before our herald could count six ; the portals
opened, and Aras, who, to his infinite delight, was
stared at by every one, was conducted into the wizard's
reception-room.

The magician, expecting some important personage,
·had thrown himself into his state chair, assuming a
most satanic expression, that he might deeply impress
the herald with his royalty. Judge, then, of his astonishment when Parry stalked in. Although greatly dis-
appointed, he was not uncivil to the Aras, and evidently
liked his brilliant uniform.

"When will my excellent visitors arrive?" he inquired.

"They only await Earl Griffin's return to Castle
Griffinstone, and will in all probability arrive to-morrow night."

Zamurungi dismissed the herald with a most gracious
smile, giving directions for his proper entertainment.
Aras was only too glad to be relieved so soon from the
presence of the illustrious barbarian.

Owl and Mouse were not so comfortably provided for as our herald. After nightfall they alighted noiselessly on the middle tower, took a bird's-eye view of the extensive palace, and then began their work of investigation. At midnight a chorus of heavy sighs, mournful lamentations, and wailings arose on the wings of the whispering winds from every block of crystallized sufferings.

The vigilant Owl and Mouse peeped in all the windows as they passed by, but they saw nothing to give them a clue of Zuleika's whereabouts. " Let us enter somewhere," said the Owl ; but this was easier said than done ; every door and window was skilfully locked. At last, flying around the belfry, they found the door of a loop-hole ajar, through which they entered. After choosing a convenient resting-place, the Owl said, " Now, Dory, you may go on a tour of investigation while I rest here ; I am very tired from this long flight, while you must be in good trim for work. Early in the morning I shall expect you back here ; mind you do not lose your way."

" All right," whispered the Mouse, bounding off in high spirits, while the Owl buried her head in her feathers, and soon fell sound asleep. Early in the morning Dory returned and gave the watchword. " Zuleika,"

5

hooted the Owl, and soon the two friends sat gossiping together. "Well, Dory, what have you discovered?" inquired the Owl. "Nothing, I am sorry to say, to further our purpose. I have seen strange and horrid sights, but have found no traces of Zuleika. Passing Parry's room, I heard him caressingly ask the chambermaid about her mistress, describing the fireworks he had seen at Griffinstone displayed for her amusement, telling her how frightened we all were. But putting her finger on her lips and one on Parry's, the girl said nothing. This is as horrid a place as Griffinstone! In one room I saw nothing but skeletons of a great variety of creatures arranged in rows, some in glass cases forming frightful avenues. Another was filled with the skins of these animals, birds and reptiles, so artfully put up that they all looked alive. Then I came to another chamber, which contained bottles filled with all sorts of uncouthly shaped things, together with snakes and worms. Another filled to the top with dried insects and shells. A large hall was crowded with live creatures stolen from all parts of the world, where I found a distant relative of mine, a little black, blind mouse; but he was as deaf as blind, therefore I could learn nothing from him. This awful wizard makes even the worms work for him; for in one apartment I saw millions of these things spin and spin until they had spun the very entrails out of themselves, when they dropped down dead in their own productions, changing to a shapeless mass. But the climax of all horrors I saw in a black chamber, in which, upon numerous benches, lay chopped-off limbs of human and animal creatures, legs of frogs and insects, human arms and birds' wings, animals' heads and fish tails, and here. . . ."

" Hush, hush, Dory; no further, or you will drive me mad with desire to see these wonders myself. What an opportunity that monster has to study, to dissect and inspect the marvels of creation! To establish such an institution for glorious knowledge in my native place, the capital of King Eagle, has been the ambition of my life. I must have a thorough inspection of this place before we leave, for I mean to carry out my idea before I die. This, my little friend, is the source from which the magician drinks the knowledge that gives him his power."

Dory was so horrified by his friend's sudden outburst of admiration for what he declared the very climax of infamy, that he took a leap of six feet to get away from him, believing that he had suddenly become insane.

"Owly, Owly, have you lost your reason?" cried Dory, in utter dismay.

"No, no, my innocent friend; but I am convinced that I would find more of it in these halls. Be a good mouse, Dory, and take me to the spot directly."

"I am glad you are not mad, my wise friend; but I never thought that anything short of the fine arts could disturb your sublime equanimity. It would strip every blessed feather from your back if you attempted to creep into those doomed chambers through the holes which I dug for my special entrance. Zamurungi is too wary a wizard to leave such places unlocked and unbolted. No; let us go to sleep, for I am very tired." And so they did.

Towards evening hundreds of imps scrambled up the belfry and commenced ringing the bells to announce the arrival of the illustrious visitors. Dory covered his ears with his little paws as far as they were able to do so, for fear of being deafened.

The wizard took great pains to please his noble guests, and had given his best rooms for their use. Monkey was introduced as court-jester, and Maggy as " Chevalier d'honneur."

Zamurungi seemed to take naturally to the Monkey, who made himself at home instantly, and played

his jokes upon every one that came in his way, without
waiting for an introduction.

When at the sumptuous supper the wizard's son did
not appear, Prince Armurat lost his appetite completely, and sat in moody silence, while Falcon had to
do all the conversation. Late at night the guests
entered their chambers, where Dory had arrived an
hour before.

Prince Armurat threw himself into an arm-chair,
exclaiming in great passion, "Why didn't that devil
of a wizard's son make his appearance? By the holy
moon! if he should be married to Zuleika, after all!"

"Calm, calm yourself, your Royal Highness; keep
cool as an iceberg, or you will betray our purpose to
the old man's many spies, by whom, no doubt, we are
surrounded," said Noblefalcon, with immovable stern-
ness.

"But where are our allies?" replied the Prince;
"have they not arrived yet? Where is Owl—where
is Dory?"

With a scrambling noise Dory appeared at the top
of a boot, in which he had hidden himself to escape the
chambermaid's eyes. "I am here," he piped, and probably fearing Noblefalcon's obliging handling, jumped
upon Prince Armurat's finger before either of them

saw how he did it. The latter, in his excited state of mind, pressed the little Mouse with such vehemence to his heart, that Dory uttered a shrill squeak, and only escaped from being squeezed to death by jumping from the Prince's caress on to the nearest object, which was Baron Falcon's prominent nose.

The stern Falcon showed no sign of surprise or indignation, but calmly lifted his right claw to remove the intruder, when Dory, in a new fright, left this seat, and in trying to reach the back of the washstand fell into the basin. There the poor creature was swimming for his life, and must have drowned had not the Falcon seized him by the tail and lifted him out of the water.

The Mouse got upon a bench and commenced drying himself.

"Well, my pet, what is the good news?" asked the Prince, hardly able to suppress his laughter.

"The latest news is that I am yet alive, your impetuous Highness. If you intend to be as civil to Zuleika when you meet her as you were to me, she may as well be killed by the wizard's son as crushed to death by you."

"Pardon," said the Prince; "come to me and I will dry you in my hands, while you give us your news."

"You will crush me again; I cannot trust you;" but

after a little coaxing he scrambled upon Armurat's finger. "Where is Zuleika?" groaned the latter.

"Here, Prince."—"Have you seen her?"

"My feet are small, and this palace like an empire; how could I?"

"All is lost," moaned the Prince; "you were my chief reliance."

"A frail support, indeed, my friend, is the life of a mouse; but, inasmuch as the tooth of one of my ancestors once liberated a lion, I do not see why I should not set a maiden free. Do not despair, Prince; one may sooner lose his head than his humor if he wish to achieve great things. But as I only came to welcome you in this uncouth place, my business is done for to-night, and I beseech you let me out now, for I want to hurry away to explore. To-morrow night look out for me again. Good night;" and off he went. But one may give a promise with the best of intentions, and yet not be able to keep it. The next night came, and the next, the third, and the fourth, but not our Dory. Was he entrapped—killed?—

Night after night the wizard arranged fresh entertainments for his guests—balls, concerts, theatricals, and mock-fights were on the varied programme. Prince and Falcon had to appear merry and delighted with the entertainment, although impatience and doubt tortured them in many ways. Monkey alone was in his element, and played his part admirably well ; he went into merry-making heart and soul, which is absolutely necessary for the success of any undertaking. He kept the magician and his court in continual roars of laughter by his humorous performances. He took every liberty with the old man pulled his beard or nose, took his toad crown from his head, put it on his own, or rather his head through it, so that the golden toads appeared dancing around his neck. Sometimes he would take Zamurungi's wand, and flourishing it around, assume the airs of the wizard, and give his commands to every one at the table, and so forth.

Maggy laid many a snare for the talkative fowls, but regarding Zuleika he could not draw out a word from the dullest of them. The Owl kept alone, pondering in the belfry, and took occasional surveys, without discovering anything of importance.

The only ray of hope left to Prince Armurat was the look of discomfort on the wizard's son's face ; he looked anything but like a successful lover, and entered into all the enjoyments with about as much zest as they themselves did. During the day he would often disappear, and on his return look more dejected than when he left, in spite of his efforts to appear merry. It was therefore safe to conclude that Zuleika yet withstood his wooing. Dory's absence grows quite alarming, and we must start in quest of him, but not unarmed, for there is no telling what we may encounter if we intend to follow in the track of a cunning little mouse.

5*

CHAPTER VI.

THE WIZARD-DANDY'S WORKSHOPS.

DORY having thoroughly investigated the large and intricate castle without finding a vestige of Zuleika, remembered his experience in Castle Griffinstone, and downward took his course. But he found it more difficult to find his way in the winding passages and labyrinth of avenues than in Griffinstone. Although here was a system, he could not find the clue. Frequently, after a long tedious walk, he found himself returned to the entrance. Discouraging as this was, he was bent upon success, and always started again with an undaunted will and perseverance, taking careful notice of every object he passed, so as to remember the route. At last he perceived a faint glimmer of light; he followed its direction, lost sight of it many times, but after a great amount of difficulty had been overcome, he confronted the entrance to a spacious vault. Thou-

sands of little creatures of indescribable shape, from
the human form down to the ugliest beasts, were
noisily working—hammering, filing, spinning, and
braiding wires, which others twisted into beautiful
ornaments ; some were scraping, others polishing the
manufactured objects. Large· heaps of glittering diamonds, burning rubies, laughing emeralds, cheerful
topazes, mourning sapphires, together with all sorts of
precious stones that were ever seen, besides silver,
gold, and other valuable metals, lay here and there
upon the floor; and dark-looking urchins were continually running to and fro, adding their fresh supplies.
Close by the entrance at which Dory had arrived, a
rather handsome young gnome was at a work-bench,
viewing a costly ring which he was about finishing.
Dory thought he would try whether the young fellow
understood the Mouse language, so he might get some
information from him concerning the object of his
researches ; whereupon, trotting up near to him, he
said, " How exquisite ! Is that your own doing, good
friend ? " But the gnome only hearing the squeak of a
mouse, seized his hammer, and throwing it at him
would have killed the little creature, had he not prepared himself for such a reception, and quickly disappeared under the bench. ·Anon a crowd of work-fel-

lows gathered around this uncivil fellow, admiring the afore-mentioned ring, upon which were to be seen, delicately embossed, the fierce wars between the ice-bears and seals among their ice mountains.

"Well done, well done, my boy," said an old man, probably the foreman of the shop. "I hope this ring will look tempting in Zuleika's dove eyes, and will be endowed with magic power to capture her heart. You deserve to be a member of the Vulcan Society for the Promotion of Fine Arts. I will propose you in our next annual meeting, when a name shall be given you." Thus saying the foreman took the ring and went toward the middle of this immense workshop, where a circular counter was erected of pure gold, the steps of which consisted of the purest garnet. A very ugly man, in whom our Dory recognized the wizard's son, sat at the desk, upon a costly embossed chair. To this incarnation of ugliness the foreman offered the ring, and, bowing to the ground, said, "Here, my lord, I deliver to you a fine work of art, such as nothing superior has left these royal works ; it is the original invention and execution of one of our most promising young men, possessed with great genius, whom I recommend to my lord's special patronage and grace."

"Dare you speak to me in this way about such clumsy apprentice-work? Am I an ignorant fool, whom you can impose upon?" cried the infuriated wizard's son. "Insolent slave! Dare you defy me, by dictating to me what I must like? This is a mountebank's production, and I despise your gray hairs for intrusting so important a work to the hand of such an imbecile; that fellow is ignorant of the first principles of anatomy. Go, fool! and have a superior work produced, or you shall be thrown into the seventh centre —food for the faithful dragon."

"Aha!" thought Dory, "the dragon—seventh centre. I am on the right road." But he had no time for further reflection, for he saw this overbearing, infuriated master seize a fiery mace, which he brandished in the air, roaring, like the eruption of a volcano:

"All ye infernal hosts, hear the voice of your master!"

As if by magic a host of armed knights appeared, and surrounding the throne, began shouting the following command :—

Silence, ye myriads!
Open your ears!
Hear, hear!

Goblins and gnomes !
Spirits of fire !
Hear, hear !

Then roared the voice of the wizard's son through the great vaults: "All ye hands of the miner's corporation, dive to the very centre of the earth and bring the costliest jewels and metals that old Chaos hoards in his treasury."

CHORUS.

Powers of darkness,
Children of night !
Dive, dive,
Down to the very deep,
Down to the dark abyss,
Dive, dive !

Break pure diamonds,
Rubies and precious stones,
Break, break !
Dig for the emerald,
Dig for the crystal,
Dig, dig !

Down into night's realms,
Down to the deep,
Plunge, plunge !
Seek for the platina,
Silver and gold,
Seek, seek !

When the last words of this exhortation had died away, the wizard's son continued :

"And you, my faithful servants of the subterranean goldsmith's corporation, I charge and command to exert yourself in producing works such as never have been seen before in beauty and costliness." To which the knights replied in the same weird chorus :

CHORUS.

Powers of muspelheim,*
Children of fire,
Work, work !
Join with precious stones
Silver and gold ;   .
Work, work !

Blow all the bellows,
Melting the ore ;
Blow, blow !
Strike ringing anvils,
Hamm'ring the gold ;
Blow, blow !

Glossy and shining,
Polish the work ;
Rub, rub !
Off swing your hammer,
Children of fire ;
Clang, clang !

* The empire of fire, where Gurtur was king.

During this strange scene every workman stood
in silent awe, with head bent to earth and hands folded
across their breast; but now the wizard ceased and
the chorus ended, the knights disappeared, and every
one hurried to his work as if spurred by whips. Clang,
clang, rang from every corner of the huge vault, the
response of anvil to hammer. Dwarfs and pigmies ran
in every direction to execute the orders of their superiors. Only the poor foreman, deeply wounded in his
feelings, made his rounds of inspection with a heavy
heart and bent body. Stopping at one of the work-
benches, where a man made an elaborate tiara, the
kind-hearted man said, "You are improving very fast,
my good lad; but take your time; pass over nothing
hurriedly." Then contemplating the tiara he added
to himself: "Zuleika, Zuleika, poor captive in the
Golden Garden, for your sake I hope that this treasure
may have power to soften thy heart toward our
master." Returning the tiara to the hands of the
workman, he said by way of correction, "Run the out-
lines of the dolphins a little clearer, and give a bolder
relief to the head of Aramandel, and give a finer curve
to the sea-horse's neck; you may also take off something of the curl on Pamolina's forehead."

"Golden Garden! that, then, is Zuleika's hiding-

place; but where is that?" Dory kept saying to himself, while he proceeded on his way. Presently he
came to a hall where a number of pretty little girls sat
cutting and stitching. Robes of velvet and silk, embroidered with gold and gems, fashioned and shaped
themselves under their tiny fingers, as if it were no
work, but all play. One of the matrons looked at a
beautiful dress, where the roses, lilies, and forget-me-
nots vied with each other in perfection, and exclaimed,
" This must be charming in the eyes of the fair
Zuleika, who above in the Golden Garden mourns in
abjectness, and win her love for our master! O maiden,
didst thou know thy fate, if persistent in thy refusal,
thou wouldst consent to-day! Stitch away, girls;
stitch, stitch!" and backward and forward, up and
down in rapid motion went a thousand needles.
" Above," repeated Dory ; " of course, the Golden Garden could not be below; but more I must find out,"
and walking or running further he came to another
great vault, when tuck, tack, tuck a hundred little
shoemakers were manufacturing wondrously fine shoes.
And after a while he heard one of the men, who took
a remarkably neat shoe from his last, exclaim, "O
Zuleika, Zuleika, would I could make this little shoe
whisper in your ear: Accept my master, that thou

mayst not be given to Chaos' own grandchild in the seventh centre. No, no. Better it is to live in the Golden Garden west of this palace, than be carried south to Griffinstone, or deep under here to the seventh centre. Tack away, boys ; tuck, tack, tuck."

"To the west of this palace lies the Golden Garden, where Zuleika is captive ; that is at least something ; but now for the seventh centre. I long to see that many-headed beast," piped the little Mouse, and he sat down to meditate. How a thing could have seven centres puzzled him not a little. At last he concluded that this phrase meant the centre of the seventh cellar, remembering that similar abbreviations are often used by common people. Besides, he had passed already through four cellars, each below the other, stretching as far as the foundation of the palace. Why might there not be seven ? He therefore descended to the fifth, sixth, and finally the seventh cellar. Here the labyrinth was laid out with even more ingenuity than in the first cellar ; but Dory would not be baffled, and he was finally rewarded by a sight which he related to the Owl, as follows :—

"Turning a sharp angle, I almost fainted at the appalling sight that presented itself. Burning streams springing from a thousand sources crossed each other in their fall in front of a cavern, where they made a river of fire. There in the cave lay the dragon, with his many heads, snorting fire at every breath. The heads were directed to all points of the compass. The tails, of which there were seven, were twisted around a dark-looking object, which I recognized as the iron-wood chest that contained the ebony heart which holds the Good Spirit captive. My dear Owly, at this sight my courage failed me ; for who of us can cross the fiery stream—pass the blazing portcullis of fire ? Who dares to encounter that beast, and where can one find weapons to fight that completely armor-clad monster ? I actually sat down crying at that sight, and the more I contemplated it, the more I became convinced that Zuleika's liberation is next to impossible."

When Dory had studied this monster to his heart's content, he retraced his steps, and his wonderful bump of locality enabled him to get out of the labyrinth in safety. In the evening of the seventh day, Dory noise-lessly slipped into the leader's room with the servant.

" I cannot possibly endure this any longer," exclaimed the Prince, after the servant left the room. " Can the spirits of midnight think of a more torturing punish-ment ? I have to laugh and talk all day, as if I were the happiest man in Asia, while a hundred passions consume my heart. Is Dory dead? has the Owl deserted us? Oh, torment of powerless inaction! how long shall I have to suffer thee? We know no more to-day than at the moment of our arrival. Everybody professes to know nothing of a maiden held captive here. And you, my cautious Baron, who always interferes, lest, as you say, I should betray us, tell me, what have we gained with all our wariness?"

"Saved our necks, which I deem one important gain."

"Had you not drawn me out of the hall last night, I should surely have cut that old hypocrite to mince meat."

"You forget, Prince," interrupted the Falcon, "that Zamurungi is invulnerable while the Good Spirit is yet imprisoned, and that he can call to his help thousands of demons as long as that ring sits upon his finger. Be patient; our time for action will come, and perhaps sooner than you imagine. I still trust in Dory, and yet believe—" "Peep, peep, peep," which means in the Mouse language, "You are quite right;" and Dory perched himself on his hind feet in the middle of the floor, and stroked his long moustaches. Who can describe the joyful surprise of the two friends at Dory's sudden appearance? and Falcon, who was nearest, put his claw forth to lift him up again; but taking a side leap, Dory said:

"Thank you, my Noblefalcon; I have just saved my

skin from being burnt to charcoal, and don't want to be
scratched by your long nails."

"Come to me, my pet," called the Prince, highly enjoying the Falcon's rebuke.

"My thanks to you also, most gracious Royalty. I
have not narrowly escaped being killed from a goldsmith's hammer, to be squeezed to death by your impetuous caresses. Give vent to all your feelings while
I sit at a distance, and when you have quite eased your
heart, I will come and tell you all I know of a certain
young lady."

"Have you seen Zuleika?" exclaimed the Prince,
bounding up like a sky-rocket, and descending upon
the floor just where Dory sat, whom he surely must
have killed this time, had he not, quick as ever, swung
himself with a skilful leap upon the top of the bed-post.

"Well, I declare," squeaked he, as soon as he had re-
covered breath sufficient to do so, "that you are the
most dangerous friend any being ever had. I seriously
advise you to find a hippopotamus to find your Zuleika,
instead of poor me. I will go home to-morrow, and no
longer expose myself to being killed by you." ·

"Really, I feel ashamed that I have allowed my passions so to overcome me. I acted like a brute. But
if you only knew, my darling, in what a purgatory of

mental agony I have been living ever since your departure, you would not reckon with me so closely."

"I cannot see how protecting one's self against being
killed can be called close reckoning," replied Dory,
quietly keeping his seat.

Armurat held out his hand coaxingly, entreating his
little pet to try him just once more; but Dory was not
so easily reconciled this time, and so he jumped high
up upon the window-sash, and addressed him thus:

"Only think, my passionate lord; if telling you that
I heard of a fair lady is enough to make you almost kill
me, what would be my fate should it ever happen that
I introduce you to her?"

"Dory, Dory, pearl of all the mice, if you do this I
promise to have you gilded all over, and put you in a
glass case studded with diamonds."

"Is that your idea? Then Zamurungi forbid that I
ever should succeed in doing so. I have lately been
weltering in heaps of diamonds and gold, and do not
see any enjoyment in it; no, I prefer my plain white
coat."

Noblefalcon's impatience grew almost beyond con-
trol, but always keeping his decorous dignity, he said,
in an earnest tone: "Here, my Mouse; this is no time
for frivolous jokes; begin your report."

"I am by no means joking, your Serene Highness, but speak in sober earnest." But he obeyed the Baron's request, and jumped upon Prince Armurat's uplifted hand, and there related his long story.

"You incomparable Mouse!" exclaimed the Prince, when Dory had finished. "How can I ever compensate you?"

Noblefalcon had no time for explanations, and immediately began to lay his plans.

"To find out the situation of the Golden Garden must be our next object," said he; "and I have just got an idea which I hope will accomplish that. To-morrow, at breakfast, we will propose a ride into the country. Methinks I have seen a dark wall standing out against the western horizon. We will induce the wizard to drive in that direction, and try to learn from him or some one of the company the object of such a construction. A satisfactory answer we cannot expect, of course ; but we have the use of our own eyes."

"Agreed; but what about the graver matter—the Good Spirit with the dragon?"

"Leave that to me, Prince; I am going to see Owly, and sit in council with him. Neither of you can do anything in this matter ; even if you could pass the fiery streams, you could never get through the work-

shops in safety, to reach the cavern. To-morrow night
we will meet here again, when I will listen to your
report. Pleasant journey, and good-night." With this
the cheerful little creature bounded off.

Mouse and Owl held a long consultation in the
belfry, but the only result they arrived at was the conclusion that all they could do was to sleep until the
following night. Next morning, when at breakfast the
day's amusements were broached, the Falcon proposed
a ride into the country, as the weather was all that
could be desired. Of course Armurat seconded him,
adding that neither the Falcon nor he had had an
opportunity to admire the beauties of that irregular
country.

The proposal was unanimously adopted, and the
carriages ordered.

Zamurungi, his son, Armurat, and Falcon drove in
one carriage. The Monkey had succeeded in rooting
himself so deep in the old wizard's affections that he
could not do without the jester; consequently he also
got in the same carriage.

After a drive of a few hours, Armurat said to his
host that he would like to have a closer view of that
dark-looking wood, so unlike anything in the country,
and asked the nature of the trees.

"What you see over there is a living wall," replied the wizard, "which I planted for the protection of my winter garden."

"Might we not drive thither?" asked the Falcon, with an air of indifference; "I remember hearing my father speak of the great Zamurungi winter garden as one of the wonders of Asia."

"Your father!" exclaimed the wizard, "did he see it? I do not recollect having had the honor of entertaining him," he added, with a suspicious look at the Falcon.

"I do not believe he ever saw it, but he could not fail hearing of a thing so famed as he said your garden was. I do not think my father travelled farther north than to Earl Griffin's castle, whose guest he was for a time," replied Noblefalcon, to allay the wizard's suspicion.

"If you will honor me with a visit in winter time, I shall take great pleasure in showing you the Golden Garden, as a great poet chose to call it, who passed a season with me hundreds of years ago. He was a highly gifted man, but probably dead now. He gave it this name on account of some very rare trees, which I succeeded in purchasing from the estate of the great Adam, who failed, as you will remember. They grew

6

in his favorite residence of Paradise, and are the only specimens saved from the deluge. These trees produce annually a crop of solid gold leaves, differing from the common gold in its tint, which inclines strongly to the green. Hence you understand why I so carefully protect this garden against intruders. I should take great delight in showing the place to you, were it not that the trees have just shed their leaves, and look barren ; besides, the green-houses are being repaired."

Our friends, of course, saw easily through all these vague excuses, but accomplished as much as they had hoped for—that is, prevailing upon Zamurungi to drive them all around this formidable wall. Noblefalcon scrutinized everything very minutely, while Prince Armurat and Monkey attracted the wizard's attention by turns.

"Blest be thou, consoling night!" exclaimed Armurat, when the two had entered their chamber again ; and throwing himself in an arm-chair he remained in moody silence for some time.

"If your Falcon eyes discovered nothing, I am sure there is no ingress through which we could hope to enter the garden. Can your brains think of anything to accomplish that end?" he asked the Falcon, after a while.

" I am afraid that the wall is not the only obstacle ; the very air seemed to be guarded," was the reply.

" How so ? "

" Distinctly I made out a vaporous something hovering over the wall and rising high in the air."

Midnight having passed, Prince Armurat became very impatient that his Dory had not arrived, when he suddenly appeared, entering through a very small door which he had contrived for himself. " Why are you so late, Dory ? We have lost patience with your tardiness," was the reception he received from the Prince.

" Then you do not surprise me, for everything and everybody moves too slow and comes too late for one who has lost his patience. Now, if I were king, I would create a new office, called the lost-patience office, with a numerous staff, appointed for life during good behavior, independent of political parties ; for I dislike the ruinous practice in King Lion's realm of removing tried and faithful officers of the public service because they do not hold the same views in matters not concerning their office as the men in power. The duties of these officials should be, to pick up all the patience lost, which is an enormous mass, and restore it to the owners. I am sure nothing would more effectually cement a throne to the rock of public satisfaction, and it would prevent revolutions as well in empires as in families. On a small scale I have introduced this plan in my own home, and I assure you we never have quarrels ; every member of my family finds his lost patience restored upon his clean plate at the breakfast table every morning. We discuss our differences with a full stock of patience, and thus harmony is easily restored. And think, good Prince, what a blessing such an arrangement would be to all rich people, and what an invaluable boon to their poor relations and heirs."

"Very good, my little friend ; I am convinced I shall have to nominate you prime-minister when I ascend the throne of my forefathers."

"My future sovereign, I have the honor to restore to you your lost patience, which your future majesty dropped a little while ago. To the King, none but his prime-minister ought to do this service."

"Incorrigible rogue !—but what news have you to tell me ? "

"Frail vanity ! I thought this was something new —but, yes, Maggy told me that by perseverance he drew from an unwary servant the confession, that there is no other entrance to the Golden Garden but through an underground passage from this palace, watched by three-headed bloodhounds." Before separating, they agreed to hold a grand council the next morning, whereto Dory summoned the whole company.

CHAPTER VII.

THE GOLDEN GARDEN.

ATER in the evening of the following day we find Dory sitting upon a stone fronting the Golden Garden. When at the last council in the Prince's chamber only irresolutions, instead of resolutions, were adopted, and one of the irresolutions was, that nothing could be done except watch for opportunities, Dory left the room with a sorrowful heart, thinking that there was something better to be effected, namely, to create opportunities. All day he spent in finding the underground passage to the Golden Garden, determined to brave the three-headed bloodhounds ; but it was all in vain.

Out of humor through the failure of this object, he went out of the palace to take a ramble in the country, when the thought came to him to go and have a look at the Golden Garden wall, and there we find him pondering.

"I will try whether I cannot cut my way through that obstacle," he said to himself, leaping from the stone to the wall, after having sharpened his teeth. With a good will he set to work; but alas, vain effort! The moment he touched the thicket innumerable dagger-like thorns came starting from every branch and leaf, burying their points in his head and body. The Mouse was not easily daunted, and renewed the attack several times, but with no better result; then he tried to leap the wall, but before he was a few feet from the wall he was obliged to throw himself over. Bleeding profusely, he was obliged to give up the attempt. Utterly dejected and much wounded, the little Mouse, writhing with pain, crept back to the stone, managed to climb it, and then sat down, wrapt in gloomy thoughts.

"What a glorious night!" said he. "The moon, radiant with smiles, sheds her soothing light over all the earth and sky, heedless whether she shines on joy or sorrow; and how the fleeting clouds chase each other in loving sport, now hiding the moon, and then dancing in a ring around her! how happy they seem! They take no thought of Zuleika, who suffers within these walls ; they care nothing about the poor defeated Mouse's agony. But are they not right? Why should they, children of light, leave their enjoyment and weep with the unfortunate, whose misery they have not the power to alleviate or lighten in the least degree? and would not their whole short existence be spent in sorrow should they condole with all the misery they see? How selfish one gets in suffering! No, no ; play on ; love and dance while you are at liberty to do so. How still is this midnight hour! No song from the happy, no curses from the wicked, no sighs from the unfortunate are heard—nothing, except my own wailings !"

Any one who had seen our Dory at that moment would have said, "Look! there's a little mouse asleep."

"Well, Dory, what is the matter now?" a voice was heard saying close by ; at the sound of which, Dory made a tremendous leap in spite of his wounds, and disappeared under the stone.

"Dory, Dory, don't you know your old friend?" cried the Owl. Hearing the familiar voice of his friend, Dory crept forth again, still trembling with fright and pain.

"How you scared me, Owly! But I am indeed glad you are here ; you could not have come at a more opportune time. How did you know that I was here?"

"That is easily explained, my dear friend. Being hungry, I went out to find some food. I had an appetite for some snake or lizard, and thinking I might find either near this hedge, I flew this way, and then discovered you in a most forlorn situation. But how you are bleeding, my dear Dory! what has happened?"

"Do you know that this is the Golden Garden?"

"Indeed you surprise me!"

"And in there sits Zuleika."

"True, if that be *the* garden."

"Well, Owly, I was trying to get in there, to see our Fairy Queen; but the moment I commenced cutting at the hedge, thousands of daggers were thrust at me; when I tried leaping the wall I was received in the same manner. It is of no use. I wish you would try to fly over it. Do try; but take good care lest you might be hit by some missile from a hidden killing-machine. I will watch here."

The Owl moved at once toward the wall, examining everything very closely with his large eyes. As he approached he noticed the same suspicious, vaporous-looking something that Falcon had observed; it looked to him like network, rising high in the air. He got a stone, and keeping at a sufficient distance, threw it with all his force against the apparent mist, when, fearful to relate, sparkling rockets were fired off in all directions from thousands of hidden batteries ; some sparks actually singed the tip of his ear. Slowly he rose higher and higher, until he had ascended more than three miles. At that height he passed the barrier, and soared above the Golden Garden. Quite as carefully did he descend, mistrusting every object, and alighted in the middle of a pathway, made by a covering of golden leaves from the wonderful trees ; the stems of these trees he noticed were silver. In the centre of this garden, surrounded by a moat filled with gold-fish, stood a tower-like building. As the rays of the moon fell upon it, the glare of the prismatic colors were so great that it nearly blinded the Owl—especially from the windows, which were made of the purest diamonds. The Owl peeped through one of the latter, and oh, joyful sight ! there lay Zuleika upon a divan, as beautiful as ever, only that grief had blanched and thinned her cheeks. The room was regally fitted up. The choicest refreshments were placed upon a sideboard. Rare flowers were placed about the room in profusion, musical instruments in the fashion of those times, besides games and other inventions for pastime.

With a cry, "The bell, the bell," Zuleika started up. "What is it? Who can it be? Can it be the monster again? But no; it rings the melody of friendship; yet what friends can come to you, Zuleika, in this satanical abode? Are you too getting deceitful, mysterious voice? Can I no longer even trust you, my only friend in all my troubles? Is the demon's power so great, or his wealth so tempting, that he has succeeded in bribing you? Oh no, no, no!" and she sat down weeping. But the bell continued merrily pealing. "Surely this must be in token of a friend at hand," said she, rising. At this moment she perceived the Owl at the window. But for the bell, Zuleika would have taken him for one of the wizard's many spies, prying in to see what she was about.

"Are you a friend from my beloved home?" exclaimed the agitated maiden, going to the window. "Do you know anything about my dear father and mother?" The Owl answered in his hooting language, but, alas! Zuleika did not understand him. He then scratched upon the window-panes with his feet and beak, to make her understand that he wanted to be admitted.

"You cannot enter," said Zuleika, perceiving his purpose; "there is no communication with the garden.

I am a close prisoner, and were it not for these open-
ings in the ceiling. made to let in the perfumes from
the garden, I should be suffocated."

Looking up, the Owl perceived at intervals small
apertures in the wall. "Good-by," he hooted, and
flew off.

"Does he understand me?" thought Zuleika, sad to
see him depart so soon.

The Mouse still sat on the stone, washing his bloody
skin, when the Owl returned.

"Get on my back quickly, and I will carry you to
Zuleika."

"Wait awhile, Owly, until my coat is clean," said
Dory, licking in great haste; and when he had made
his toilet he did as he was bidden.

The Owl stopped with his rider in front of the ven-
tilators, telling him to jump off; but before Dory did
so, he said in an entreating voice, "Owly, dear friend,
promise me faithfully to wait outside until I return,
else some mishap may befall me."

"Trust me," he answered; and off his back through
the hole the little creature leaped, right into Zuleika's
lap. She was surprised, but not alarmed, for the bell
had been ringing its merry peals.

"You are a friend also, my little Mouse, and I have

small cause to despair while my friends thus increase in number," said she, stroking Mousy's fur. "But what message do you bring?"

Dory knew full well that she did not understand his language, consequently speaking to her would be loss of time; therefore he decided to try the pantomime again, through which he had so well succeeded with Fatima. In an admirable way he imitated all the gestures of a frantic lover; greatly improved by his late practice at Griffinstone, he did it so well, that Zuleika, who at first became frightened, thinking the Mouse had got into fits, broke out into a loud laugh, exclaiming, "Is it possible, that you have seen that wretch of a wizard's son kneel before me in his foolish style? It must be so, or else you could not imitate him so well. The impudent villain yet dares to persist, although I have told him that I would sooner die than consent to marry him. But, alas! he has even wrung from me the promise, by means of the most diabolical threats, to become his wife, under the condition of his men executing certain things, which I mean to make impossibilities." The well-known clink of the bell suddenly terminated her soliloquy.

"Oh, horror and dismay! the monster is coming; there is no peace for me night or day. Be quick, little thing ; hide thee in my sleeves, or your white skin will soon be placed among his large collections."

Dory had hardly time to nestle himself close to Zuleika's snow-white arm, when a painful discord, produced by various unmusical instruments, announced the arrival of the wizard's son. Twelve odd-looking men in grotesque dress preceded this dreaded personage. Each one of these little men carried a present for Zuleika upon a velvet cushion of various colors. They had received orders to kneel in a semicircle, and at a given signal lifted the presents above their heads.

With measured pace, and, as he fancied, majesty, strode the wizard's son into the captive's room. Exactly half way between the door and Zuleika, he stopped and bowed slightly ; after which he stepped forward, seized the maiden's hand, kissed it and pressed it to his heart with a groan, rolling his greenish-yellow eyes. After this performance he beckoned to one of the men to bring that coronet which Dory saw in the workshop. It was really the finest work that ever left a goldsmith's hammer. This he placed upon Zuleika's head. Calling the second, he took from him a magnificent necklace, with a locket in which was his portrait ; he threw this upon her neck in such a manner that the locket came right over her heart. He was delighted with the idea of being near Zuleika's heart, if only in a miniature. The third man brought that ring which had caused him to call upon the whole infernal regions for more effectual exertions ; this he placed upon her finger. Dresses, shawls, shoes, and in short everything to complete the toilet of the most fastidious belle, was laid at her feet. This done, he motioned to the dwarfs, and they left the room in a jumble. Torturing his voice into a tender accent, the lover addressed Zuleika in the following words :—

"Goddess of my heart, sovereign ruler of my soul, upon my knees I implore you to accept these gifts from the hand of your servant, and yield to his wishes."

" If I am your goddess and queen, as you repeatedly assure me, why do you not obey my commands, and carry me back to my parents ? " replied Zuleika. " As to these presents, which in your eyes seem to be works of high merit, it is humiliating beyond all measure for me to think that the great Zamurungi's son should hold my love so cheap as to try buying it with such baubles! I have told you, and repeat it, that my love cannot be bought at a cheaper rate than that of any

princess of Asia, poor unprotected girl though I
am. And I wish you to understand, that, unless you
offer me gifts of such beauty as human eyes never
looked upon, I must decline your offers of marriage."

"Do not push your obstinacy too far, adored fairy,"
resumed the wizard's son, in a bitter-sweet voice;
"many a young maiden has repented, through a long
life's suffering, the obstinate refusal of devoted love.
Remember, queen of beauty, that the patience of the
mighty is soon exhausted, and that—revenge is sweet.
To-morrow I will come again with yet more costly
presents. My people do their utmost to please you.
Farewell, then; but, Zuleika—remember!"

Moving his mouth in an effort to produce a smile
he again seized Zuleika's hand to kiss it, when suddenly Dory, unable to suppress his wrath, leaped from
under Zuleika's sleeve, and buried his sharp teeth deep
in the cherry end of his nose.

With an oath that made Zuleika shiver like an
aspen leaf, the wizard's son released her hand, and
with a quick motion caught poor Dory before he had
time to extract his teeth. Zuleika looked with dismay
for the immediate death of her friend; a slight squeeze
with that hand would send the heroic soul from the poor

little Mouse. But Dory did not give him time to do this, but bit so deep into the wretch's thumb that his hand loosened its grasp for half a second, but long enough to give Dory time to escape, and hide himself among the despised gifts. With curses too shocking to repeat, the wounded lover trampled the costly things, until they presented nothing but a heap of rags, unaware that the Mouse had slipped away into a bouquet of flowers.

Finding that he had not killed the little animal, he searched all over the room, but with no better success. "By the powers of earth and old Chaos, that insignificant beast shall not escape me!" he roared, and opening the door he thundered into the subterranean darkness: "Brutalu, Bestialang, my faithful dogs, quick; here is work for you to do!" In stormed two monstrous bloodhounds, with three heads each.

"Hunt, catch, kill that white mouse," he commanded; and they eagerly set to work, answering with a howl of approbation.

They soon found Dory's hiding-place, and almost swallowed vase and flowers in their eagerness. The poor little fellow had to run hard for his life. The brutes upset and tore everything he chose for a shelter.

Zuleika once tried to snatch him from under their jaws, pretending to save a costly box, which they were in the act of upsetting ; it nearly cost her her hand, but helped the Mouse to escape. The wicked wizard, holding his bleeding nose with his left hand, cheered the beasts with the right, highly enjoying the race. They became so infuriated that Zuleika feared her own safety, and jumped upon the divan, with her back close to the wall, trembling for the life of her little friend. Alas ! now they have caught him ; poor fellow, how he screamed ! But he managed to escape again, leaped over their heads, and almost flying across the room, climbed up on Zuleika's dress. She, perceiving his intention, lifted both her arms, screaming fearfully with all signs of terror. Quick from her arm to her hand, and from there leaping through the square hole under the ceiling, he jumped upon the watchful Owl's back, who landed him in the belfry, while his persecutors looked for him in the moat outside.

"That I call a narrow escape. I had already given you up as lost," said the Owl, while putting down the Mouse.

"So it was indeed, my friend. But didn't I punish him ? He will feel those bites a long while. And now let me thank you for the promptness with which you helped me ; without your help I would be dead by this time."

The Owl took the grateful friend under his wing, and both sat down to sleep.

When the Owl thought it was time for the Mouse to report to his superiors, he gave Dory a pinch, which awoke him. After a long yawn and a good stretch, Dory gave his hands and face a thorough washing, and then set off. Knowing what he had to relate, and having grown cautious through experience, he carefully climbed upon a bracket above the chamber door, and then said, in his shrill voice :

"Good evening, my impetuous Prince and my stern Falcon ! "

" Where are you, you rascal ? "

" Higher than your Highness can reach."

" Come down."

" I shall take good care not to do so."

" You certainly have news to tell ; be a sensible Mouse, and come down. I am dying to hear what you have to say."

" I have much good news to tell you, therefore I came here ; but I shall by no means come down before I have told you all the horrible things which make you so desperate."

"Nonsense, Dory ; try not to torment."

"Well, then, hold yourself in readiness, while I fire off my first shot—I have seen a certain young maiden ! "

"Seen Zuleika !" cried both at once.

"Yes, I have seen her, and she is as beautiful as ever—perhaps a little thin from sorrow. Prepare for the next volley—I have kissed a certain maiden."

"Pilfering wretch !" groaned the Prince. "Come down instantly, that I may make you give me those kisses."

"Thank your, Royal Highness, they are quite contented to remain with me. Now bang goes the third —I have slept upon the arm of a certain maiden. Oh, how round and soft it was, Prince ! "

"Proceed, tantalizing creature ; tell what you know at once, and in a concise manner ; you are pricking me all over with needles."

"Well, that will give you an idea of the sensation I felt a few hours ago, only pins are daggers to me ; but attention while I pull the trigger for the fourth shot—I saw a certain young man kneel before a certain young lady ! "

"Wretch, keep to the truth ! Say you did not see it, and were only joking ! Dory, don't turn a hair in order to make your narrative more interesting," groaned the Prince, turning very pale.

"Believe me, it is exactly what took place ; but here goes the heaviest missile—I heard a fair maiden say if this young man would bring her presents such as no human eye has ever seen, she would accept his love ; but that she was by no means to be bought cheaper than any princess in Asia, or rather that her love couldn't be."

"Monster!" burst out Prince Armurat, completely losing his composure ; and he strode up and down the room, heaping maledictions first upon Dory, then even upon Zuleika, and lastly, most cordially, upon the wizard's head.

The roguish Mouse sat chuckling out of harm's way, and quite enjoying Prince Armurat's outburst of jealousy.

"Prince," said he, after a while, "good-night. I shall go and take a nap until the tempest of your temper subsides ; but do not storm too long, for we have much urgent business to do, and let me give you a little dose of comfort. When that interesting young man took the lady's hand to kiss, I leaped from under her sleeve and bit his nose so deeply that it will take some time for it to heal. It nearly cost me my life ; I never ran such a race before."

This was soothing oil upon the tempestuous sea of Armurat's rebellious passions. Sunshine returned to his face, and Dory could leave his elevated position in safety, and, perched upon the Prince's hand, he related the dangerous events of that memorable night.

It was agreed by the three assembled conspirators that Armurat should write a note to Zuleika, similar to the one to Fatima. The note ran thus:

"Fair Zuleika, friends are working to effect your liberation. Keep up your courage, preserve this secret, and hold yourself in readiness.

"PRINCE ARMURAT AND NOBLEFALCON."

Dory took the note in his mouth and hurried up to the belfry, mounted upon the Owl's back, and sailed swiftly through the air to the Golden Garden. He threw the note into Zuleika's lap from one of the holes under the ceiling, stayed only to witness her emotions of joy at the sight of the words, and after making some signs of endearment to her, sailed back again to the palace, softly bedded in the feathery cloak of friend Owl.

The following evening was to be the climax of Zamurungi's unbroken efforts to amuse his guests. He had long resisted their repeated entreaties to give them proof of his reputed power in necromancy. However, being assailed again, in a moment of excellent humor, brought about by a new performance of Monkey's, he consented, and appointed the next evening for that purpose.

This evening—that is, the one previous to the performance—our friends withdrew early, pleading indisposition on the Prince's part as an excuse. The Baron had whispered to Monkey to follow them to their apartments later in the evening. They set their brains to work to devise plans for immediate action. Falcon announced that the time for action had come, and that their utmost energy would be taxed. Monkey was anxiously looked for, but midnight arrived before he made his appearance. At last he came with many excuses, saying he could not help having a lark with Parry, who came across him on his way up; that they had had great fun. "You are not summoned here for fun, but for serious business," was stern Falcon's salutation. "All right, all right; do not look at me as if you wanted to find out what I have eaten for supper, or rather, been drinking. To be serious, I must have fun first. Now give me my instructions, and I swear, my lord, I will act as if it were the jolliest joke," replied Monkey, seating himself flat on the floor.

"Your inclination for intoxicating drinks will send you to the madhouse ere long," said Armurat, suppressing his laughter at the jester's inimitable grimaces.

"Oh, ah, bah! I think I am there already," was his answer, while coolly sucking his thumb.

"No more of your jesting now," said the immovable Falcon; "listen to what I have to say. You know Zamurungi will give a performance to-morrow evening, and we intend to give one in return; in this, our performance, you will take an important part. I expect we shall see some wonderful sport to-morrow night. You know the wizard's chief power lies in the possession of that ring, which you must have seen upon the first finger of his left hand. To-morrow night is our opportunity, and we must take the best advantage of it to liberate our beloved Zuleika. Monkey, I want you to watch studiously for the first moment you can snatch that ring from Zamurungi's finger, and quickly give it to the Prince. The old villain is very fond of you, and suspects everything in you is a trick; therefore it will be easy for you to playfully take his hand."

"But how can you overcome Zamurungi before the Good Spirit is liberated?" asked Monkey.

"Owl and Mouse will act in concert with us. They have concocted their own scheme, and seem confident of success. But much will depend upon good luck; yet daily experiences assure us that confidence and a strong will, together with a good cause, have insured success to still more perilous undertakings. Leave us for to-night, but look in during the forenoon to-morrow; perhaps we may have something to add to your instructions," concluded the Falcon.

Very early the next morning, when all the inmates of the castle were quietly enjoying their morning dreams, the Owl awoke Dory with a slight scratch of his claw, saying, "Dory, the time has arrived that we should do our work. Never mind washing yourself so carefully," he added, when he saw how Dory, as usual, set to work to the cleansing operations which often occupied him a long time; "we will have a great deal of dirty work to do this day, and of a kind to make you look more like a sweep than a page."

"Owly," said Dory, "let us postpone our work until to-night; I should like so much to see the mighty wizard's performances and tricks in the black art. I have never seen anything of the kind before. Say, friend, have you no curiosity? What harm can it do if the Good Spirit remains a few hours longer in the wooden heart?"

"Dory, Dory, never let your curiosity overcome

7

your sense of duty," replied the Owl, gravely. "I shall begin to think less of you if you say one word more on the subject ; hasten, and let us be off."

And off they went for the seventh centre. It was easy enough for Dory to slip along unnoticed when they arrived at the vaulted workshops, where the clang of the hammer was heard every hour of the twenty-four, but it was less so for the Owl. He had to watch his opportunity very carefully, and by fits and starts dart through these large subterraneous halls, filled with thousands of beings, of whom any one might kill him with some tool or other, if he was not very cautious and swift of wing. Hammers, files, tongs, footstools, and precious stones were flung after him from all directions by shouting crowds of juveniles. At last they arrived safely in front of the chamber of horrors. It always remained a point of dispute with them who was the most frightened of the two. Dory said that the Owl's feet and beak turned sky-blue, and Owly maintained that the Mouse's nose became ash-colored.

Allow me to pause for a moment, my young friends, and contemplate the situation of these insignificant weak creatures. Remember, they had come here of their own free will, neither by order nor compulsion, nor stimulated by the hope of rewards. There they stood in front of that hideous monster, supported only by moral strength and the ardent desire to serve a good cause, which cause was to liberate the wronged and oppressed, to crush the black empire of evil by liberating the spirit of virtue and freedom. Remember how completely removed they are from the support of their friends. Behind them has closed the empire of brutal force; before lay that hideous monster, ready at any moment to annihilate them; no sympathizing friends to encourage them; alone, they confronted overwhelming dangers.

While they sit there, collecting their strength and maturing their plans for action, we will return to the palace and witness the performance in the black art.

CHAPTER VIII.

DORY'S TRIUMPH.

DINNER was over, the dessert cleared away, and the wine was doing its duty of making everybody merry. Monkey, who on this occasion was joking with a purpose, even surpassed himself in his clownish frolics.

Suddenly a voice, not unlike the moaning sigh of an American bull-frog, sounded through the hall: "Attention, my good friends!" When quiet was established, Zamurungi murmured a few unintelligible words, waved his wand as if drawing figures in the air, and suddenly appeared, nobody could tell where from, a number of pigmies, dragging a huge kettle, headed by a band of torch-bearers. These halted in the middle of the room and threw their firebrands together into a heap; five thin and wiry gnomes jumped into the fire, forming a pentagon, upon which the kettle was placed. Into this kettle each gnome threw a diminutive golden heart, and at once a beautiful girl rose from the steam and flew into the arms of the pigmy who had thrown a heart into the caldron.

When every one had gone through this ceremony and received his bride, they commenced dancing around the fire in the wildest glee, singing the following wild, ringing song :

> Hasten we all
> Quick to the call !
> Master commands
> All to a dance !
> Come springing !
> And singing !
> Come leaping !
> And creeping !
> Join all in a dance,
> The master commands !
>
> Light as the wind,
> Fleet, fleet as the hind !
> Quick as the stream !
> Swift as the beam !
> Come jumping
> And thumping,
> Come rapping
> And tapping,
> Join all in a dance,
> The master commands !

At the conclusion of this song the wizard turned the ring on his finger inward, and the noisy imps disappeared, leaving no trace behind. He turned the ring outward, murmured a few words, and an enormous platform arose from the ground, a mass of blue fire bursting from its centre. Right and left of the fiery column appeared two brazen hobby-horses. A man, stately and lordly, seated himself upon the one to the right; a woman in rich attire seated herself upon the one on the left side. The magician's wand described some figures in the air, whereupon the man opened his mouth, and a dove flew out of it right into the flames; then the woman opened her mouth, into which the dove already roasted disappeared. Dove after dove escaped from the man's mouth, passed through the fire, and vanished, nicely roasted, in the same manner. He was rapidly fading away, while she seemed to enjoy the feast with unceasing appetite. When nothing but a skeleton was left of the man, they both plunged into the flames with a shriek, and in an instant innumerable little imps made their appearance on the top of the fiery column, dancing and whirling around in gleeful antics. Inward turned the ring, and they too vanished. After this the magician called two knights up—one in golden, the other in silver armor. After the customary formalities of a fencing match had been gone through, they commenced cutting at each other in furious earnest, their swords piercing the metal plates most marvellously, and severing limb after limb from their bodies. But oh, wonder! Each limb, as it touched the platform, grew into an armor-clad knight, who fiercely set upon his opponent. By this means the whole stage was soon crowded with golden and silver clad warriors, hacking each other mercilessly. Suddenly a slight move of the conjurer's wand set them laughing ; they threw down their arms, shook hands, and embraced one another.

Inward moved the ring, and off they flew like chaff before the wind.

It may be as well to mention, that the ring on the conjurer's finger had the power of calling forth, and commanding to disappear, any number of goblins in whatever desired shape, but the wand alone controlled their actions ; therefore the one without the other was almost useless.

With a tremendous thunder-clap, that almost deafened the Prince, and made the Falcon exhibit a passing emotion of fear, and which sent Monkey shivering under the wizard's wide garments, appeared a host of dragons, lining the whole wall, and showers of many-colored fire-rain came pouring from their nostrils. These fiery sparks gathered in rings about the heads of the spectators, whirling in rapid motion around them. At a given signal, all the dragons loosened themselves from the walls, and darted like lightning towards the platform. There they huddled in a mass, with their heads outside, and assumed collectively the appearance of a pyramid burning with phosphoric light.

This blunted pyramid was surmounted by a sphinx. Presently, at Zamurungi's command, this was changed to a golden altar, on the top of which appeared an image of a calf, cut out of a single diamond.

And now the room was alive with all sorts of uncouth creatures, which, in the air and on the platform, commenced dancing as only goblins know how, everyone shouting and croaking far beyond his size.

"Treason, your Majesty, high treason!" was all at once heard distinctly above this deafening din. Everybody believed this to be part of the play, but when the threatening form of Earl Griffin appeared in the middle of the hall, they knew it was sober earnest.

"This lotus, mighty Zamurungi," continued the Griffin, holding a leaf of this plant high in the air, "was discovered to-day behind the seat in Fatima's cell, by the porter, while sweeping the apartment. Fortunately I was at home. Fatima persistently denied knowing anything about it, but your ingeniously contrived instruments of torture soon made her confess all she knew. It appears that a little white Mouse [how lucky for friend Dory that he was not present at the show!] was sent by a sympathizing friend, [looking significantly at the Prince, who felt his blood curdle]. On investigation, I learned that this creature found its way through the apertures for ventilation, which fact ought to be borne in mind. The treacherous little vermin was the bearer of this despatch from the sympathizing friend to Fatima. Herein the friend promises her liberty and restoration to her parents if she will give such information concerning you, powerful Zamurungi and Lady Zuleika, as to insure success to their plans. The postscript, to destroy this lotus-leaf effectually, was neglected. Was there ever a greater proof of falsehood and treason! I see that you are amusing yourself and these honored guests with theatrical performances; why not close it with a drama, and have these villains dragged upon the platform and executed on the spot?"

Scarcely had the Griffin mentioned the little Mouse's visit to Fatima's cell, when Noblefalcon saw that the wizard's son left the hall in great haste.

While Zamurungi, in utter surprise, was attentively listening to Earl Griffin's accusations against his guests, the Monkey playfully seized his left hand, and drawing it under the folds of the wizard's garments, succeeded in pulling off the ring. With a sudden leap he stood at the Prince's side and put it on his finger, whispering a few words to him.

"Take those two miscreants and throw them into the seventh centre, welcome food for the dragon," shouted the wizard, waving his wand. Instantly the entire host of demons burst forth with a terrific howl, preparing to execute the order. But when just on the point of seizing them, the Prince waved his hand which contained the ring, crying, "Ho! ye all, obey my command!" (This was what the monkey had whispered to him.) In less time than it takes to tell it, the immense hall was cleared of every living being but Zamurungi, Earl Griffin, Prince Armurat, Noble-falcon, Monkey, Parry, and Sir Magpie.

"Villain," roared the conjurer, in extreme rage, "you have stolen my ring! Death to you." And flourishing his sword he leaped upon the Prince. Armurat, fully prepared, warded off the heavy blows which the wizard showered down upon him. It was a sight that every lover of the art of sparring and fencing would have enjoyed.

Prince Armurat felt that his case was hopeless.

He knew that he could not kill nor even hurt the wizard, and would have been overcome had not the ring invested him with additional strength. Monkey tried to wrest the wand from the magician, but without success. He received a thrust from his sword finally that sent him bleeding to the other end of the hall.

While this combat was going on in the upper end of the hall, a tremendous fight took place in the lower part.

"Prepare for death," shouted Earl Griffin; "thy father was a nobleman and my honored guest, but thou art not his true son. I have sworn to imbue my hands with thy blood."

By such taunts the Griffin thought to goad the Falcon into an attack upon him; but he was too wary; he did not reply a word, only watched his opponent narrowly. Suddenly the huge dark mass of the creature came rolling upon the Falcon like a thunder-cloud.

Falcon, swift of motion, whirled him around like a whirlwind, and buried his beak so deeply in the Griffin's neck that blood flowed freely and a close wing-to-wing fight ensued. It was a grand spectacle to see these lords of the mountains wrestling in close quarters, making no sound save the flapping of their huge wings. Noblefalcon's youthful agility was his sole support in this otherwise unequal combat, but he felt that his power of motion diminished every minute from loss of blood. Maggy and Parry did their best to assist the Falcon, and annoyed the Griffin considerably ; but they could not materially affect the struggle. While they fight, we will take a look into the seventh centre, and see how our friends there are getting on in their undertaking. They seem yet to be staring at the many-headed engine of death.

"Your last idea is not so bad," said Dory ; "it might succeed, but will take too long a time ; think of something better."

"I know that these fiery streams are a great obstacle, but Dory, I say, the only manner of getting at the right is to run through all the wrong ways you can think of."

"What an odd philosophy!" replied Dory ; "quite like your whole tribe of profound wisdom-worshippers! But oh, dear Owly, look at the monster! Every head looks like a huge cat, with all sorts of frightful ornaments on it, ready to leap upon you." And, poor thing, he really shivered all over from fear. It is but justice to say that Dory was naturally not very courageous, but though a coward by nature, he became a brave hero by philosophy. "I have got an idea, Owly, which must succeed," continued the little Mouse. "You go as near the cave as the fire will admit, and keep the monster steadily in your eyes, and so keep yourself in his. I will hide myself under your feathers, and when you are near enough, creep out behind you, and begin digging into the earth. Our sole endeavor must be to prevent the monster from detecting my action; should he suspect my doings, we may make our last will at once." Taking another long look at the monster, he added, "Owly, what a luxury it is to gaze at one's misery!" And then he covered himself completely with his friend's ample feathers.

The Owl went as near as he could venture to be safe from scorching, and then sat still, staring hard at the monster. Dory slipped off behind, and set to work scratching and digging like a good fellow. His greatest difficulty was how to get rid of the loose earth. Fortunately, after digging down a few yards, he crossed the bed of a dried rivulet, in which he might empty all the refuse. Carefully had he taken notice of the relative localities of the fiery stream, and was guided in his course by the heat from above. Thus he knew precisely when he arrived under the Dragon's ring.

To determine the exact locality of the chest was

more difficult; he must dig upwards to ascertain its position. Having failed in his calculation, he broke the surface under one of the dragon's tails, which he scratched with his blunted nails.

A tremendous roar from the three times nine throats shook the seventh centre to its foundations, and caused Owly to make a complete somerset, who was at that moment trying to find out whether that monster belonged to the class of mammalia or reptilia. Dory, however, had learned what he wanted to know, and he soon felt the chest with his digging nose.

From this he gathered fresh courage, never thinking of his dangerous position; he gnawed and cut in such earnest at the hard wood of the chest, that he several times broke the edge of his front teeth, and had to sit down repeatedly to sharpen them again. At last he got through the wood of the chest, and there lay the heart. What joy for the little Mouse, to be so near the end of his dangerous task! He wanted to jump about in the dark chest, but he feared lest the monster might hear him. "Now for that sham heart," thought he; and again he sawed away eagerly, with newly sharpened teeth.

Ebony is very hard, and it will take the Mouse some time to break through that thick wall; so we shall go and see how Zuleika is prepared for the emergency.

She sat upon her divan, lost in contemplation of the mysterious announcement upon the lotus-leaf; who was this Armurat? She did not remember having heard his name before.

Presently the bell announced the arrival of an enemy. "The fiend," she exclaimed; and, hiding the leaf, tried to look composed while she took up some flowers to arrange. "He said he would bring new presents to-day, but marvellously beautiful though they will be, they are not good enough to win me, and never shall be." But instead of the formal announcement and procession of present-bearers, the wizard's son rushed in without ceremony.

"Where is that white Mouse?" he cried, and seizing the girl by the arm he tore her violently from her seat. "Where is the infamous beast that was here with you yesterday? did he bring you a message also? Give me the leaf. What does it contain? what is your sympathizing friend's plan against us?" Thus heaping question upon question, without waiting for an answer he flung the trembling maiden back upon her seat. This violent motion caused the leaf to fall from her sleeve on to the floor. Taking it up in haste he read it. "Ha, ha ! to liberate you is their plan, is it ?—to steal you from my grasp ?   Poor imbeciles, whom the monster is despatching by this time ! Now, Zuleika, no sympathizing friends will ever again try to liberate you ; therefore choose at once between marrying me to-day, or being taken by Earl Griffin to his castle, where you will find suitable company for an obstinate woman, blind to her own interests.   Your cell will be next to Fatima's, and your name 102."

"Send me to the dungeon at once," answered Zuleika, in a feeble but firm voice. At this juncture a snake came twisting and sliding into the room, and winding herself up to the infuriated lover, hissed something in his ears.

"What ! " he exclaimed ; "my father's ring stolen from his finger, and all the servants gone except the Griffin ?   And he and my father in deadly combat with the villanous guests ?   Loosen the blood-hounds, and follow me, ye legions of the Vulcanic corporations, to the grand hall !" shouted the wizard's son, while he disappeared in the labyrinth.

Come, let us hasten also, and be present at the scene of strife that must ensue when he arrives.

Prince Armurat's strength is failing fast on account of the many wounds he has received, while Zamurungi

has not got even a scratch ; he fights on nobly, however, but against hope. Another thrust, and oh,
wonder ! a stream of dark blood gushes from the
magician's arm. "Murder ! I am bleeding ! By old
Chaos, the spirit, my mortal foe, must have escaped from
the false heart !" cried the magician in boundless rage.
This exclamation threw the Griffin off his guard for a
moment, giving the Falcon an opportunity to bury his
beak deep into his flesh. Armurat gathered his remaining strength, and aimed a thrust that would have
finished the old wizard, had not his son appeared at
this moment with his forces. Perceiving his father's
situation, he leaps upon the Prince, and catching his
arm ere he is aware, cries in his ears, " Yield yourself
prisoner, or these hounds shall tear you to atoms
instantly !" Prince Armurat, sure that his friends have
liberated the Good Spirit, thinks time gained is everything saved, throws away his sword, and surrenders
himself prisoner to his rival, and so does the Baron to
the Earl. The old necromancer snatches his ring from
Armurat's finger with such haste that he almost broke it.

The wizard's son then gave orders to tie the captives
to the back of his two favorite blood-hounds, and to
carry them to the Golden Garden, where he will pronounce their sentence.

This accomplished, all the assembled rabble follow the leader to the Golden Garden, roaring and shouting along the vaulted road.

The mystic bell was in a feverish state of excitement all the time, alternately ringing sweet music and pealing mournful dirges ; and poor Zuleika wandered up and down her golden prison in an agony of fear and hope.

Now she catches the distant howl of the multitude and the infuriated beasts, that long to devour their burden. The noise increases, and the crowd have arrived at her door, which flies open, and her persecutor enters, closely followed by the hounds with the prisoners tied to them. " Here are your sympathizing friends, Zuleika," grinned the wretch, pointing to his victims ; " they want *your* sympathy now. Their intention was to liberate you, but now it depends upon you whether you will liberate them; the tables are completely turned ; speak their sentence. Will you now consent to marry me, and see your partisans loosened from the animals and sent back to their homes ; or do you decide upon their destination by refusing me? They shall in that case be devoured before your eyes, and after that I pronounce your sentence—that is, to be shut up in cell 102 at Griffinstone Castle, for the re-

mainder of your life, which will be ten times as long as
it naturally would be. Make your choice in haste."

Poor girl, had she any choice to make? Had the
question simply been to marry this monster or go to
the dungeon, she would not have hesitated, but would
have chosen the latter. But to see her friends killed
on her account—that she could not consent to, and
therefore said :

"Hear me, most powerful sir! Since the lives of
these two noble beings, which were so gallantly risked
for my sake, depend upon my choice, I declare that,
compelled as I am, but not by free-will, I will marry
you."

"You will not," called a stentorian voice. "How
happy I am to be in time to prevent you binding yourself to that wretch, who now shall receive his reward."
Thus saying, the Good Spirit entered in all his serene
majesty, and released the prisoners.

When we left Dory, you remember, he was gnawing
in high spirits at the ebony heart. The moment he
succeeded in breaking it the wound in Zamurungi's
arm proclaimed to our friends the successful operations
of the Mouse. Though free, the Good Spirit had to
subdue the frightful dragon ere he was enabled to
leave the cave ; and what a gigantic combat it was !

Owly always said he should never forget it in all the days of his life ; while Dory used to say he could never have believed it possible, had he not seen it with his own eyes.

Scarcely had the Good Spirit succeeded in killing the monster, when Zamurungi himself came rushing through the dark avenues, followed by his legions of demons, who in obedience were bound to the ring he had snatched from the Prince. The Good Spirit by this time had roused his own followers and allies, and then such a fight ensued as had not been heard of since the Archangel Lucifer himself battled with the legions of heaven. Owly and Dory hid themselves as well as they could in a corner. When the whole infernal army were routed, driven to precipitate flight, Zamurungi fell like a weak old man into the dust at the Good Spirit's feet.

"Unfortunate being," said the Good Spirit, "whose only pleasure in life was to create misery and sorrow for your fellow-creatures, reap the fruits of thy sowing. Henceforth, forever remain captive in this same cave, where thou hast held me for ages !" He dragged the powerless wretch into the cave, rolled a huge block before the opening, and sealed it with his ring. This done, he hurriedly called the Owl and Mouse from their hiding-places, and arrived, as we have seen, just in time to save Zuleika from pledging herself to the villanous wizard-dandy.

"Your punishment, weak-minded wretch," said the Good Spirit, addressing himself to the latter personage, "shall consist in being forever hunted through these dark avenues by your own favorite hounds, who will take care that you do not suffer from idleness." Seizing the shivering dandy, he thrust him into the dark, crying, "Fly!" Then he drove the hounds out after him, commanding them, "Hunt!" And the walls of the labyrinth re-echoed the yells of the pursuing beasts.

The vast structure of the magnificent palace, solely erected of tears and sighs, dissolved into airy clouds, fragments of which long lingered on the horizon, illuminated by the rays of the full moon.

Everything had disappeared, except Shuhu's airy car, in which the Monkey, the Aras, and Sir Chattering Magpie were found hidden, convinced that this was the beginning of the last day, and they had resolved to die together in the car. The foxes alone remained calm, and patiently waited for the arrival of their masters.

The Good Spirit joined Armurat's and Zuleika's

hands together, saying, "Take her, Armurat; you have well deserved her by your valor and perseverance. And you, fair maiden, will surely be happy with and make happy your liberator. Remember, at the birth of your first-born I shall come to see you again. But now off for Griffinstone, where some work yet remains to be done."

Clapping his hands, a beautiful chariot appeared, drawn by four white swans. You, Armurat and Zuleika, take seats in this; and you, Noblefalcon, occupy your car with the rest of the company. Zuleika begged to have little Dory with her, which of course was granted.

After smiting the monsters at Griffinstone, the Good Spirit opened all the dungeons. Fatima he gave into the charge of Armurat and his bride, with directions to restore her to her parents.

Shaking hands with all, and especially thanking Dory for his undaunted efforts to release him from captivity, he wished them good speed. Earl Griffin had made good his escape to the North Pole, where he possesses the Castle Crystal Rock.

At the frontier our heroes separated. Noblefalcon had to report to King Eagle, while Armurat with the two maidens drove to his father's palace. Zuleika's

eyes were filled with tears when she had to take leave
of her dear Dory. Fatima wept also. They begged
him to go with them, but he declined, being anxious
to see his wife and little ones. He promised, however,
to come with his family, and make their palace his
home as soon as they kept house for themselves. It
was hard to part with the bright little creature, and
Zuleika literally covered him with kisses. Prince
Armurat wished to kiss him also, but he respectfully
refused, saying he wished to keep Zuleika's kisses for
himself. Then he quickly took his comfortable seat
upon Owly's back, and off they sailed.

CHAPTER IX.

THE MYSTIC BELL.

THE old king's court was thrown into great commotion when Armurat arrived with his lovely bride. There was great rejoicing, fro the throne down to the lowliest cot. The gray-bearded monarch received Zuleika as became a princess, as he thought she was. How could he think otherwise? She had beauty sufficient for a princess, and manners good enough for one. Certainly her dresses, made by the wizard's most skilful workmen, were costly and elegant enough for the richest of royal maids, and above all she was good and cheerful enough to be a king's daughter. The tree of her ancestors grew in his imagination until it reached with its roots to the deluge.

After dinner, when the ladies had retired, the king

and his son remained talking over their wine. The old man listened to his son with rapture, while he related his manifold adventures.

"My dear father," said Armurat, after a pause, "I cannot deceive you; my Zuleika, the most royal of maidens, is no princess."

"What! no princess?" cried the old king, in utter surprise.

"What I mean to say is, that her father is no king, nor her mother a queen; in all else, I think she is as complete a princess as any in Asia."

"But, Armurat, what do you mean by this? Zuleika no princess; then again she is a princess, but her father no king? Has the wine affected your head? I understand you are joking in a merry hour, to see how I would receive such a revelation; but, my boy, I dislike such folly. Playing with royalty is a dangerous affair."

"No, father, I do not speak lightly. Zuleika is the daughter of poor and honest people."

"Then she must leave the palace at once!"

The Prince did all he could to appease the old man's wrath, but in vain. He persisted in saying that his son should never marry any one but a real princess, and ended further discussion by telling him very curtly to go to bed.

Zuleika overslept herself the next morning, partly from fatigue, but chiefly from indulging until far into the night in those waking dreams so fascinating to maidens engaged to young and handsome lovers.

Zuleika, living in charming dreams, did not therefore witness the discordant scenes at breakfast the following morning. The old man would not forgive the girl for not being a real princess, and threatened to disinherit Armurat should he persist in marrying her. To assure his father that the Good Spirit himself had given her to him, was of no use. The queen remained neutral for some time, to see which of the two would be the winning party; so when she saw how firm the king stood she sided with him, thinking that would settle the matter.

Prince Armurat grew very sad; he loved his parents too well wilfully to cause them any pain; but his love for Zuleika was supreme. At this moment of agitating suspense, Zuleika entered the hall, robed in all the loveliness of a bride. The king arose abruptly to withdraw, but Zuleika advanced towards him respectfully, to kiss his hand. Rudely he pushed her back. The poor maiden stood all amazement; what had she done to offend her father-in-law, who but yesterday received her with every mark of affection? Her eyes filled with tears, and she looked upon him with the mild reproach of wounded innocence ; it seemed to rivet him to the spot. A strain of plaintive music was softly wafted through the morning air, and as its melancholy waves touched the ears of the king, he was fettered as by magic.

Timidly Zuleika drew near him and grasped his wrinkled hand, her tearful eyes looking sadly into his. But he shook her off again, intending to roll an avalanche of reproach upon her ; but the words died away in an inaudible murmur.

" What unaccountable music ! Whence come these mournful tones ? " whispered the king, moved by the strange sensations that crept into his heart. While his eyes wandered about to detect whence the music came, they met the dark-blue eyes of Zuleika, that in angelic purity rested upon him. He strove to free himself from their charm ; but as the disturbed needle of the compass, swinging right and left, soon returns again towards the point of attraction, so came the king's eyes back to those soul-reflecting mirrors.

By a mysterious power he felt attracted to the maiden before him ; he advanced a few steps, yet his pride forbade him to obey the promptings of his feelings.

The bell rang louder, with tones of heavenly music, filling the air with its harmony. A fierce contest between the deep-rooted pride of an eastern prejudice and true nobility raged in the king's breast, and was reflected in his face. An unseen power, as it were, pushed him forward; he halted, struggling with an invisible opponent. With a sudden effort he rushed forward, and clasping Zuleika in his arms, wept like a child.

The following day was agreed upon as the wedding-day, and the whole capital was set in motion to complete the extensive preparations, even the king and queen taking active part in it.

Zuleika was therefore left to herself, and enjoyed the day as best she could. She went down to the yard to take a look at the splendid elephants and horses in the royal mews; then she looked into the poultry-yard, where she was deafened by the cries of welcome which greeted her, while the hens all went to work to lay eggs for her. From thence she naturally directed her steps toward the garden, and from the garden to the fields. She was very happy, and the mystic bell in her bosom was sounding forth soft peals of music. As she walked on, the birds and little animals flocked around her to do homage to their queen. She nodded to them with her winning smile, and took some of the prominent ones, such as the nightingales, oreoles, and swallows, into her hand, putting their bills to her lip. The trustworthy friend in her heart told the nature of the newcomer to all, so no formal introduction was needed. The lilies and violets that saw her approach, quickly spent their whole store of delicious perfumes in token of their love and admiration. She culled a pure white rose, the lovely emblem of pure womanhood, and fastened it in her bosom. At once she was startled by a peculiar rustling sound, as if winds were rushing through the leaves and flowers, although not a breath was stirring the air. She looked up and around, and was surprised to see all the flowers nodding their heads and clapping their leaves in enthusiastic applause. Then she turned her steps homeward, and her heart was full of heavenly peace, and a fervent prayer for the happiness of every created being.

With all the splendor of Oriental ceremony were the lovers married, and it was so arranged that they should pass their honeymoon with Zuleika's parents in the secluded valley. To describe the joy of these two simple people at the arrival of their child in royal state, would be vain to attempt. They were running about in the most frantic state of mind, and could say nothing but "Bless me! a real Princess, a real Prince!"

Sir Chattering and Lady Magpie had preceded them a few days to the secluded valley, to announce to all Zuleika's natural friends her return with her husband, Prince Armurat, heir to the throne of India. King Eagle at once decided upon a royal reception, which was to surpass the seventh birthday as the rays of the imperial sun surpass the silver ones of the princess moon. . . . . On the birthday of an infant prince the Good Spirit kept his promise, and visited our royal friends. He came without any pomp or announcement. His servant carried a crystal box, containing some presents for the young prince. On opening it the mother found in it a precious talisman to insure the child a good heart and a wise head.

Will he not give beauty also to his godchild, thought Zuleika, carefully searching the casket; but there was no beauty. Several times she was on the point of asking the Good Spirit for such a gift, but when she met his earnest, benevolent eye her courage failed her.

That Fatima was married to her Amadelulu follows as a matter of course; it would have been cruelty not to unite them after so much suffering.

Our friend Dory received a tiny house, nicely furnished, situated in the park, which King Eagle presented to Zuleika, and in which Armurat had

erected a splendid palace as a birthday present for his
bride. It is said in the chronicle from which this story
is taken, that Dory lived to such an extreme old age
that he turned ebony black, with not a single white
hair in his fur, and when he died Prince Armurat
had a marble monument erected in his honor. The
pedestal was ornamented with colossal statues, in
niches, of Noblefalcon, Owly, Monkey, Maggy, and
Parry. On top of this pedestal was a beautiful colossal
statue of little Dory, sitting on his hind legs gnawing
away at a heart, and upon the pedestal were the following words engraved :—

> "Here lies the gallant little Dory,
> Whose valor won immortal glory !
> Clear was his head, his heart was good,
> And firm he in all dangers stood !
> Though small in body, great in soul,
> He moved events by wise control !
>
> "O stranger ! pause here and reflect
> What feeble means the gods select
> To strike the evil that deny
> The heavenly gods' authority.
> And think, that there is power in all
> To do the good, in great and small !"

Well, my little folks, this ends the story, and our
ramble through the dingy chambers into which Father

Time throws all the murky rubbish when he orders a house-cleaning and whitewashing, to commemorate a new era. You may now go home and tell your friends what a good brave little creature old black Dory was, when he was a shining white mouse. Now let us all join hands, give three cheers for our little Dory, dance around in a circle, and sing the mosquito song :—

" Tingle, tingle, tingle,
    In company and single !
    Sing the joy of little fairy,
    Sleeping in the blooming prairie !
    Tingle, tingle, tingle,
    In company and single !"

www.ingramcontent.com/pod-product-compliance
Lightning Source LLC
Chambersburg PA
CBHW020227030726
47497CB00009B/2987